THE BURNT TOAST B&B

HEIDI BELLEAU
RACHEL HAIMOWITZ

Riptide Publishing
PO Box 6652
Hillsborough, NJ 08844
www.riptidepublishing.com

The Burnt Toast B&B

Cover art: L.C. Chase, lcchase.com/design.htm
Editors: KJ Charles, Carole-ann Galloway
Layout: L.C. Chase, lcchase.com/design.htm

ISBN: 978-1-62649-217-2

First edition
January, 2015

Also available in ebook:
ISBN: 978-1-62649-216-5

THE BURNT TOAST B&B

TABLE OF CONTENTS

CHAPTER ONE

Derrick recited the order to himself as he clattered around his parents' cramped kitchen: Two plates of eggs, one of them scrambled and the other soft-boiled. Four slices of toast, all whole wheat, one not buttered. Four slices of bacon. Two sausages. Hash browns . . .

Shit, hash browns! He'd forgotten all about those. Cursing a blue streak, he added another fry pan to the already-crowded stove. His scrambled eggs looked discolored and thin, nothing like the fluffy yellow clouds his mother used to make. He gave his unevenly cooked sausages a quick roll in the pan, bacon fat spitting back at him as he did, and then hurried to the freezer for the bag of preshredded hash browns.

Sure, his mom used to grate fresh potatoes by hand in the mornings before any of the guests were awake, but Derrick wasn't his mother. Wasn't even his father, who'd known his way around the kitchen, even if he hadn't done much cooking himself. The guy could at least fry bacon, which was more than could be said of Derrick and the shriveled black strips sizzling and smoking away in his pan.

It was almost a good thing that the Bayview B&B was underwater, because if Derrick was this stressed cooking for two guests, how in the hell could he hope to manage a full house? And as soon as he was done here, he'd have to wash their dishes, then head upstairs to strip their bed and clean their toilet. And dust. And vacuum. Not to mention the yard work and the bills and his own laundry.

What the hell was he doing with his life?

Burning toast, apparently. His two orders of whole wheat toast were as black as his bacon—he never had figured out how to cook it in the oven, and hadn't had the money or give-a-crappery to replace the broken toaster.

He wasn't meant for this. Waiting on people, cooking and cleaning, playing happy homemaker. It was all wrong. He was thirty-five, for Christ's sake. He was supposed to be working for the logging company he'd escaped to the moment he was legally old enough to get a job outside the damn B&B, except by now in a management position. Working in camp all week, coming home to his own place—hopefully with a housekeeper—on the weekends. Hooking up with younger guys whenever he was in town and feeling the itch, and never having to worry about anyone seeing or hearing anything they didn't need to see or hear. *Especially* not paying guests with access to online review websites. That was supposed to be his parents' problem.

A glance at his father's battered watch told him his guests had been waiting in the dining room for nearly half an hour. Half an hour with nothing but a couple glasses of orange juice and a pot of coffee to tide them over. He grimaced at his burnt toast and bacon. Slimy scrambled eggs. Sausages so dehydrated they were starting to look like pepperoni sticks.

At least his hash browns looked okay—but then, it was pretty tough to screw up anything frozen. Could you buy frozen scrambled eggs? He dumped the hash browns and sausages onto two plates, left the bacon in the pan it was stuck to, tossed four fresh slices of bread into the broiler, and took a plate in each hand. He could bring them *something* to eat while he tried to figure out the rest of their meal.

Staring down at his handiwork, he couldn't help but remember his mother's breakfast plates, hot and artfully arranged, with little tomato flowers for decoration. Bowls of fresh fruit salad and perfect sunny-side-up eggs. Fresh-squeezed juice and French press coffee.

Of course, back then, guests had paid more than twice the price Derrick now charged.

Too bad he couldn't just say "You get what you pay for," to every guest who complained about his subpar hosting abilities.

Instead, he forced what he hoped was an apologetic smile onto his face as he carried his two pathetic plates into the B&B's dusty dining room.

Which was empty.

His guests' table was abandoned, their drained cups of juice and mismatched coffee mugs the only sign they'd been there at all.

"Hello?" Derrick set their plates down on the table anyway. "Breakfast's ready!" He eyeballed his sad selection of food. ". . . Kind of."

"Out here!" a woman called from the front room.

"Oh, uh, okay," he muttered, picking up the plates. No, wait, that was ridiculous. If they wanted to eat, the plates would be right here waiting for them in the dining room. He set them back down again. Straightened his shirt and smoothed his hair, then headed in the direction of the voice.

His guests, a middle-aged couple indulging the wife's rabid *Wolf's Landing* obsession on their road trip down the West Coast to Vegas, were standing with packed suitcases by the front desk. The wife flashed him an uncomfortable smile. "We've . . . actually decided to find our breakfast elsewhere, if it's all the same to you."

"Uh, of course," Derrick said. Now what did a good host do in a situation like this? He'd spent so much of his childhood being teased for working here—*Playing maid with mommy again, Dicky? Bet you make a real ugly girl in that little black dress*—that he'd frankly blocked out everything he'd learned about running this place. Assuming he'd ever learned anything in the first place . . . "Right! Well, uh, there's a couple of places in town I can recommend." Now, to think of where they were and what they were called . . .

"That won't be necessary," the husband announced. "In fact, we're checking out early, aren't we, *dear*?"

His wife winced like he'd pinched her. "Yes, that's right."

"So you won't be needing the room till . . ." Derrick slipped behind the desk, scrutinizing the big binder he used for bookings. ". . . Friday anymore?"

The husband's eyes narrowed. "No, we won't be. We're checking out. Right now."

"It's just," the wife tried, "there's a nice chain hotel on the highway that's much more convenient—"

"Don't lie to the man, Helen." Her husband gave Derrick a hard stare. "My wife doesn't want to offend you, but the way I see it is, you're a professional, right?"

A professional fuckup, maybe. Derrick nodded mutely.

"Well then, let me just say from one professional to another: just because you own a big empty house in a tourist destination doesn't mean you're remotely qualified to charge money for accommodations."

Ain't that the truth.

Derrick rubbed the back of his neck sheepishly. "You're right. I'm sorry. I'll rip up your check, okay? Your stay's on me."

Helen looked like she was about to protest, but her husband took her by the arm and turned her toward the door before she could. "You think about what I said," he lectured over his shoulder, then gestured to his two suitcases, still sitting on the floor by the desk. "You can at least bring those out to the car for me."

"Of course," Derrick replied, because lifting heavy things, well . . . that was maybe the one single part of running this B&B he wouldn't screw up.

The fresh air he got just from walking his former guests' bags to their Toyota did him a hell of a lot of good, so after the car pulled out of the driveway, he only returned to the house long enough to grab his coat and keys.

Professional, hah. Derrick didn't belong in a cramped kitchen playing maid. He was meant to be out here, in the open air.

He breathed it in: cool and green and a little bit damp, like it might rain later. The B&B was uphill from main street, on the outskirts of town, nestled in a dense overgrown forest cut through by a single paved road, a few old homestead properties, and a whole maze of trails—some of them man-made, but most the narrow kind worn in by deer. Derrick followed one of the deer trails because he didn't feel like coming across any well-meaning neighbors walking their dogs. Or worse, Hollywood folks on their morning jogs. Not that they'd try to make conversation with a grizzled meat-eating mountain man like Derrick, but the fewer reminders of their invasion, the better.

Not that he was one of those types who hated change. He wasn't even one of those types who hated "outsiders" as long as they didn't give him good reason to. It was just . . . The presence of producers and actors and stagehands and gaffers swarming through town reminded him of everything he'd lost. His old job, his old life. It wouldn't be so bad if being laid off hadn't coincided with the arrival of *Wolf's Landing*. Wouldn't even be so bad if, after being laid off, he'd found another *real* job instead of getting stuck running the floundering B&B.

His parents had been so excited when they'd found out the show would be filmed on location. The B&B had been struggling for years, and they'd been looking forward to all the guests the show would bring to Bluewater Bay. Especially after Derrick had lost his job, because they'd thought it would provide him with some much-needed financial security.

So much for that, eh, Mom and Pops?

God knew why they'd ever thought that in the first place, given how obviously unhappy he'd been about his responsibilities there as a kid.

Considering the direction of his musings, it came as no surprise when his hike took him through the woods to a familiar, manicured clearing. Bayside Ridge Cemetery, with its gentle slope and sliver of water view above the trees. Derrick dusted his jeans and straightened his coat as he made his way between the gravestones. Bluewater Bay had been around since at least the 1920s, so its graveyard was a mishmash of crumbling old crosses and glossy granite stones. Derrick knew the names here almost better than he knew the names of the living people in town: Amelia Schooler, 1931–1994; Walt Gibson, 1904–1964; Delilah Shaughnessy, 1975–1990; old bird Norma Bell, 1896–1980; Baby Boy Jameson, born and died November 6, 2001, his grave site still covered in teddies and toy cars.

Michael and Shannon Richards.

He crouched in front of their headstone, carefully sweeping away a couple of fallen leaves atop it. "Uh, hey," he said. "I'm kinda running your business into the ground. I burnt the breakfast this morning. It was a mess. The guests ended up checking out early, but not before giving me a lecture." Stupid, to talk to a gravestone. Stupid and cliché, and yet, Derrick was beginning to realize he'd come down here this morning for a reason. That reason was permission, and since he couldn't call a family gathering in the living room the way he'd done when he'd first lost his job, this would have to suffice. "The husband was real mad. He said I was in the wrong business. And I . . . I kinda agree. You know how sometimes people tell you you're useless and all it does is get your back up and make you wanna tell 'em *Fuck you, what do you know*?"

He could practically hear his mother's reply: *Language, Derrick!*

And his father's, too: *For Christ's sake, Shannon. He's a man. Men swear.* And then, *Dick, don't swear in front of women. Especially not your mother.*

Derrick smiled wistfully. "Well, this time I didn't feel that way at all. And now that I'm here, I'm kind of thinking maybe it was a sign. I gave it a try, you know I did. For you guys, I tried. I'm just not cut out for it."

He wished they'd reply, even just the ghosts of their voices in his head, but there was nothing.

No refusal, but no permission, either.

You're a man now. Time to make your own decisions.

Leaving things up to shit like "signs," begging his dead parents for approval . . . Why bother with any of that? It didn't seem like the actions of any grown man.

He didn't want to run the B&B anymore, so he shouldn't. That was the honest-to-God straightforward truth.

So why didn't he feel more confident in his decision?

Maybe because in this case, being a man meant not being a good son.

Well, tough. Why should he have to be a good son to parents who weren't even here? He'd spent his whole life being a good son, spent *years* getting up to do laundry before school and coming home to chop wood and mow the lawn and fix leaky toilets after. He ought to have been relieved of all good son duties on the rainy night he got the call from the Washington State Patrol telling him that his parents had flipped their SUV. That was three years ago—three years now he'd been running this place, or at least *trying* to run it, on his own. It seemed to him, in light of everything, that he'd gone above and beyond.

"Sorry," he said as he stood, even though logically he'd talked himself into not being sorry at all. He patted the gravestone. His eyes tingled, but he didn't cry.

Which was okay, apparently, because just then the world decided to do the crying for him: without warning, the gray sky overhead split at the seams, drenching him with rain in an instant.

Derrick was a seasoned enough outdoorsman that he could normally get out of the rain before it fell, but he'd obviously been too distracted to catch how fast the sky had darkened or how the sounds of the forest had changed, or the nearly imperceptible electric shift of the barometric pressure. Too late, he pulled his hood up. "Better get going," he said, then turned and jogged back the way he'd come before the trail could get too mucky.

He'd tear the half-rotted B&B sign down on his way into the house. Maybe if he got back quick, it would still be dry enough for kindling. He'd need a fire today just to get the chill out of his bones, not to mention to satisfy the urge to burn the B&B's ledgers and his final guests' check.

Too bad. He really could have used that money. He'd have to hit the pavement hard if he hoped to find real work before his funds dried up. Mountain man he might be, but that didn't mean he wanted to rely on firewood and hunting to eat and stay warm.

He was feeling pretty settled with his choice by the time he made it back to the B&B, but he didn't get to rip out the signpost like he'd planned to.

Because there was someone standing on his front porch. A young man, barely out of his teens by the look of him, wearing an unzipped leather bomber jacket and soaking wet from his sopping brown hair to his battered suede boots. As Derrick drew closer, he could see the kid was shivering, hugging himself one-armed, his other arm in a cast half-tucked into his open coat.

A huge Army green duffel bag lay at his feet.

"Hey!" the kid called once Derrick was within earshot, flashing him a wet, toothy smile. "Any room at the inn?"

Well, Dick, you did *ask for a sign.*

Derrick gave his head a shake and trotted up to the house. Good son, bad son, good host, bad host, there was no way he could leave anyone that inappropriately dressed out in the rain.

CHAPTER TWO

Ginsberg should have caught a cab or bummed a ride. That much was obvious now. Hard to think straight, though, when he was still smarting from losing the use of his bike. But standing here on the rickety whitewashed porch of Bluewater Bay's Worst B&B—as voted by the internet—soaking wet and shivering, had a way of rearranging one's priorities.

The guy coming up the driveway now didn't look too happy to see him, scowling out from under his jacket's hood, but he hadn't gone full redneck and shouted *Get off my property!* either.

Ginsberg forced his frigid lips to smile.

"The hell are you thinking, dressed like that?" Grizzled and Grumpy scolded, but still stooped to pick up Ginsberg's bag for him.

Ginsberg shrugged. This wasn't exactly the time or the place to defend his carefully curated fashion choices. "Vanity?"

His host snorted. "Well, get inside and I'll start a fire. Get you warmed up."

When he opened the door, though, it seemed there was already a fire going somewhere, because the smoke alarm was wailing, and the front hall of the house was filled with a haze of blue smoke.

"Fuck!" Ginsberg's host stormed inside, boots trailing mud.

Wherever the fire was, it obviously *wasn't* in the fireplace where it belonged. Ginsberg chased him inside.

"Fuck! Fuck! Fuck! Fucking oven! Fucking stove! Fucking breakfast!"

The kitchen, then. Ginsberg followed the sound of cursing into a smoke-filled kitchen, where his host was struggling with a dusty fire extinguisher. Across from him, a pan on the stove top and the oven door were billowing smoke. A mess if Ginsberg had ever seen one, but nothing warranting a 911 call, either.

"Give me that," he commanded, loudly to be heard over the alarm, and snatched the fire extinguisher from his host's hands. A quick check of the pressure gauge, and he pulled his sopping wet undershirt over his mouth and nose, yanked the extinguisher's pin, took aim at the stove's burners, and pulled the trigger. As Ginsberg neutralized the fire on the stove top, his host dragged a footstool to the center of the room, where the smoke alarm was mounted on the ceiling, and knocked the battery free.

Sudden silence, and a thick blanket of white powder coating the stove top. Ginsberg kicked the smoking oven shut. Turned the whole damn thing off.

After setting the fire extinguisher down, he gave his forehead a swipe with his good arm. Didn't know whether he'd wiped away rain or sweat. "Well, that was fun."

His host blinked at him in shock, coughed, then headed for the kitchen's small window to open it. "Good thing you were here. I got no idea how to use one of those things."

"I've got a fair amount of experience with fire," he said, scrutinizing the extinguisher's paper tag. "We're lucky it even worked. The thing's expired."

"I didn't know they did that."

"I guessed as much." He put out a hand. "I'm Ginsberg, by the way."

"Derrick Richards." The other man took Ginsberg's hand in an easy, powerful shake.

"So how about that fire?" Ginsberg asked, forcing himself to let go of Derrick's big hand. "The one you were planning on setting on purpose, I mean?"

They hung around the kitchen a few minutes more, just until Ginsberg was sure the fire in the oven was completely smothered and Derrick deemed it safe to replace the battery in the smoke alarm, and then they headed through the B&B's cluttered but quaint dining room and into a similarly decorated sitting room.

Derrick may not have been handy with putting out fires, but he clearly had a knack for getting them going, because after a couple minutes crouched in front of the fireplace, a cheerful little blaze was already warming the room. Ginsberg, not wanting to ruin the dilapidated old sofa with his wet jeans, sidled up close to the flames and peeled off his coat, laying it out flat on the hearth to dry. He bent his head toward the fire and scrubbed his hand through his hair, sending water droplets flying.

"I'll . . ." Derrick muttered, "I'll just go get you a towel, then."

"Thanks."

Ginsberg stayed close to the fire—where he was simultaneously too hot *and* too cold, shivering *and* steaming—while he waited for Derrick to return. He sure hoped the guy had a room available, because while the fire was definitely a nice thought, the sooner he could get out of these wet jeans, the better. A hot shower with a plastic bag to wrap his cast in wouldn't go amiss, either. Or a cup of coffee. And since he was already standing here wishing for things likely not to be provided by Bluewater Bay's Worst B&B, why not add a back rub, a shot of whiskey, his very own pony . . .

He was still chuckling to himself about his unflagging optimism when a threadbare towel dropped on top of his head, partially obscuring his vision.

"Thanks again," he said, towel-drying his hair before moving on to his shoulders and arms. "Do you have a blow-dryer, just on the off chance? My hair's . . . particular. I cringe to think of what it looks like right now."

"Rooster," Derrick replied.

The guy's expression was totally flat. Ginsberg had no idea whether he was joking or not, and it kinda felt like the social equivalent of a mouthful of metal fillings and tinfoil. He cleared his throat, draping the towel over his shoulders, suddenly glad he hadn't taken his tank off. It might be completely see-through and sticking to his skin, but it was a layer of *something* between him and this inscrutable, hulking man.

Derrick cleared his throat too, studiously looking at anything that wasn't Ginsberg. "So, *Giiiiinsberg*. Seattle, or LA?"

"Huh?"

"Which is it? You're obviously not from around here, so are you from Seattle, or LA?"

"Oh! Neither, actually. I—"

"So you didn't hitchhike here?"

Ginsberg shook his head.

"And you're not one of those *Wolf's Landing* people, either?"

Yikes. He'd read that this guy didn't have the best customer service, but this was getting downright uncomfortable. "Would that be a problem if I was?"

Derrick shrugged. "Their money's as good as anyone else's, last I checked." He paused, peering at Ginsberg through eyes narrowed nearly to slits. "You *do* have money, don't you? Well, you're not a hitchhiker, so you must."

"I am so lost right now, dude. I feel like I'm missing an entire line of thought from you here."

"That's how I feel about your hair. What is that, some new kinda mullet? How come it's long on top but shaved on the sides? Your razor run out of batteries?" He gestured to his own utilitarian hairstyle.

Ginsberg ran his hand self-consciously through his 'do and spat out, "Hardi-har-har. That's rich coming from you, Mr. Lumberjack chic."

"I *am* a lumberjack."

"A lumberjack who also runs a B&B?" Ginsberg teased, and realized he really *was* teasing. He *liked* this guy.

"Would that be a problem if I was?" Derrick mimicked, his imitation of Ginsberg's voice all high and squeaky.

Okay, maybe "liked" was a bit premature. Ginsberg scowled. He didn't have to take this shit. He wasn't homeless . . . at least not exactly. He still had options, anyway.

"Sorry," Derrick said, and he did have a genuinely chastened expression on his dumb rugged face. "I'm pretty bad with people."

"Says the man working in the *hospitality industry* . . ." Ginsberg sighed. He turned, pointing the soggy denim sticking to his ass toward the heat of the fire. "But apology accepted."

"Okay, well, the way I see it is, you've got a pretty, uh, distinct look. I figured you were either a crusty hitchhiker type, from Seattle in other words, or that this whole thing—" he gestured vaguely at Ginsberg, which Ginsberg took as a reference to his sense of style "—is some kind of ironic fashion statement. Which would mean you were here working on *Wolf's Landing*. So, Seattle or LA," he concluded.

"That's a pretty common misconception, actually. A good portion of the production staff hasn't even *seen* California. Me, I'm from all sorts of places—"

"So you *are* one of those *Wolf's Landing* types."

"Well, yes."

"Why didn't you say so in the first place, then?"

"I dunno. You were giving off those 'kill all outsiders' vibes everybody on the crew's always complaining about."

"Oh for God's sake." Derrick rolled his eyes. "Just because we don't like your big-city fair-trade all-organic diet fads and your packs of wild paparazzi roaming our streets doesn't mean any of us wanna *kill* you."

"That's what I'm always trying to tell everyone else working the show. You know, stop acting like an outsider, and people will stop treating you like one. That's my philosophy." His chest had puffed up like a preening bird at that last bit, and he coughed, embarrassed. "But the way you were looking at me there for a couple minutes, I was starting to wonder if I was wrong."

"Well, you're not. So you gonna check in, or what?" For a second, Derrick's suspicious expression switched to wide-eyed and startled—almost adorably open—but then he shook his head and everything was back to normal. Except for the little bit of ruddiness in his cheeks. "Whole place is empty as of this morning, so you got your pick of the rooms." He seemed almost mad now, but Ginsberg got the sense it wasn't with him. Well, who wouldn't be mad about having a failing business? "Price is sixty a night, but I can do two-fifty a week or six hundred a month if you're looking for something long term."

Which was exactly why Ginsberg had moved out of his roommate's chic, pricey downtown loft and come here instead. Bad reviews or no, the Bayview B&B was a cheap, local roof over his head until he could get this cast off and back to work . . . if his job would even still be available to him then.

"And you'll cook me breakfast every morning?" he asked, trying to make his voice optimistic in the hopes that the rest of him would follow.

"Be careful what you wish for," Derrick replied darkly.

"Does that apply to my wish for a hair dryer, too?"

Derrick's reaction surprised him: the morose looking guy cracked a smile. "Don't worry your fluffy duckling head, kid. I'm sure my mom has one lying around here somewhere. Curling iron too, if you want one."

Ginsberg, feeling infinitely more comfortable with Derrick by now, just stuck out his tongue.

CHAPTER THREE

What the hell did you just do? Derrick thought as he lugged Ginsberg's duffel bag up the stairs, leading him to one of the B&B's single rooms all the way up on the third floor. The attic, really, though it'd been converted to three guest rooms for as long as he could remember. It was drafty and the windows were small and the roof was low, and maybe Ginsberg would decide that a three-story walk-up to shit accommodations wasn't worth it and would just leave. Because yeah, Derrick could use the money, but not this way, not right after he'd decided to shut the place down. He was about to implode from the twin forces of regret and self-recrimination.

"You don't get your own bathroom," he said as he squinted and fumbled to stick the old skeleton key in the smallest room's lock. He hadn't been up here in at least six months, and he'd frankly forgotten how dark the hallway was with only a tiny attic window at one end. Somehow all three hall lights had burnt out. He'd have to fix that ASAP. Sure, he wanted the kid gone, but he didn't want a lawsuit from the kid breaking his other arm tripping in the dark. "But since this place is empty 'n likely to stay that way, it's pretty much a nonissue. My room's on the ground floor, and I got my own bathroom, so we shouldn't cross paths naked at any point."

Which was too bad, because bad haircut or no, that see-through wifebeater and those skinny jeans didn't leave much of Ginsberg's body to the imagination, even in the too-dim hallway, and Derrick liked what he saw. Liked it a lot. Especially that perky little bubble butt—

And that kind of thinking was exactly why he was in this fucking mess. Less than an hour ago he'd been at peace with his decision to finally give up on the Bayview B&B, but one soaking wet outfit later, he was taking on a long-term lodger.

He was never going to be rid of this place. This lodestone around his neck, heavy with guilt and failure and grief.

He shouldered the sticky door open and led Ginsberg inside, flipping on the light switch to augment the thin sun from the low attic windows, and downright disappointed to find it working.

With Ginsberg's LA/Seattle fashion sense, he looked completely out of place in the room, which was done up in Derrick's mother's down-home decorating style: all floral wallpaper and handmade quilts on the bed and hazy watercolor art hangings. Derrick handed him the key and gestured around the room. "You gotcher bed, TV, telephone—long-distance calls are extra—uh, and there's a closet . . ."

"It looks great," Ginsberg said, dripping with what was shaping up to be trademark optimism.

And lying, obviously.

"We'll see if you're still saying that tomorrow morning, after a night on this mattress," Derrick muttered. The thing hadn't been replaced in at least fifteen years. "Also the windows are painted shut to help with the draft. Sorry they only come up to your knees, but this used to be the attic."

Ginsberg dropped onto the end of his narrow bed, yanking his ankle-high boots off and making himself at home, not even bothering to ask for a different room despite knowing the whole place was empty. It made Derrick anxious. This was not how today was supposed to go, not at all.

"You talk like you're trying to convince me not to stay here," Ginsberg said, peeling off his socks and wiggling his toes.

Now there was a thought. Just because Derrick had agreed in a moment of weakness to allow the hot city boy to stay here long-term didn't mean he actually had to live with the consequences of his decision for anywhere near that amount of time. All he had to do was convince Ginsberg of what this morning's couple had already discovered: that even a week in the Bayview B&B was too long. And for that, all Derrick had to be was his usual charming, competent self.

And if that failed, well, then he'd just have to man the hell up and tell Ginsberg to leave.

He could do that, right?

Right.

Mind decided, he shut the kid in his dark little room and left him alone to stew.

Trying not to look too carefully at the claustrophobic little space Derrick had dumped him in, Ginsberg finished stripping off his wet clothes, then rooted in his duffel for the plastic bag he'd been using to cover his cast in the shower—which, hey, was wrapped around his old roommate's blow-dryer. Ginsberg definitely hadn't packed that, and it made him grin to think of his roommate slipping the going-away present into his bag.

He grabbed the blow-dryer and his toiletries kit, secured the plastic bag on his arm with a rubber band, and then streaked naked down the gloomy hall to the bathroom—he was too stiff and tired to bother putting on clean clothes just to take them off again ten seconds later, and he *was* alone up here, after all. *And no wonder why*, he thought as he nearly went flying over the edge of the worn hall runner in the dimness.

And *then* he nearly went flying over the edge of the tub when the nice hot water he'd managed to coax out of the rattling old pipes went ice cold.

He'd barely turned the hot tap a fraction of an inch before it went burning hot.

Lovely. Back to cold, then. At least that wouldn't cause any new injuries to contend with.

Five minutes later, teeth chattering and limbs stiff, Ginsberg clambered out of the ancient tub-shower and wrapped one of Derrick's ancient shredded towels around his waist. Clearly, the taps here were going to take some getting used to from an operations standpoint. Either that, or Ginsberg was going to have to make a habit of taking baths. Quite possibly the *Little House on the Prairie* way, by lugging kettles of boiling water up two flights of stairs from the kitchen.

Well, he'd lived rougher than this. He'd make do. And having his own place, even one with a lumpy bed and barely any light and a malfunctioning shower, would always be better than returning to his couchsurfing habit.

Turned out there was one benefit to a shower without heat: no fog on the mirror. Nice not to wait around, or do that useless mirror-swipe thing that usually hindered more than it helped. Unabashedly posing for his reflection, he combed his wet hair back, then plugged in his blow-dryer, which set off an alarming amount of sparks until he yanked the plug free by the cord. Damn, it was a wonder this place hadn't burned down before now. An incompetent cook *and* out-of-code electrical?

But hey, his own bathroom. That was a new perk, and a particular pleasure for someone of his physical configuration. Speaking of which, he was getting to the tail end of his two weeks between T shots. A little topical booster to take the edge off wouldn't go amiss. He combed his hair—which had indeed looked remarkably birdlike before his shower but was distinctly better now, despite the lack of hot-air drying—then rooted through his toiletry bag for his T gel. A quick smear of that, and he moved on to washing his hands and face and brushing his teeth.

Funny how the simple joy of being able to brush his teeth never seemed to get old. He was definitely chilly, looking forward to getting dressed and possibly returning to Derrick's fireplace, but the whole ritual of cleaning up and getting presentable made him feel so human and so at home that it was totally worth the cold.

He was still going to ask Derrick for some pointers on how to operate his shower, though. And maybe to get the wiring fixed before he started a fire *outside* the fireplace.

Derrick had left the third floor sooner than was probably polite. He hadn't even told Ginsberg what time breakfast was in the morning. Ah well. Just one more reason on the big heaping pile of reasons for Ginsberg to bail.

Rudeness was one thing, but actual danger was another entirely, so after checking to ensure his kitchen wasn't still on fire and making a halfhearted attempt to clean up the suppressant powder, Derrick grabbed the footstool still sitting in the middle of the kitchen, and headed to the supply closet to dig up his toolbox, a dusty old box of lightbulbs, and his headlamp.

Hopefully all those dark fixtures were just burnt-out bulbs. Or at least nothing more serious than a busted fuse—that he could fix in minutes. But worn-out wiring would at best be hours of work and at worst beyond his skill set. And he couldn't afford an electrician; if it was something he couldn't fix, he'd have to move Ginsberg down to the much more hospitable second floor.

Ginsberg's door was half-open when Derrick got up to the third-floor hallway, but he didn't allow himself to think about what Ginsberg might be doing in there. Or to say hello. He wanted him gone, after all, not getting friendly. Besides, Ginsberg was being awfully quiet. Maybe he was sleeping.

Instead he flipped off the hall light switch, plunked down the footstool, strapped on his headlamp, and unscrewed the first dark bulb from its fixture. Shook it by his ear and let out a relieved sigh when the broken filament rattled inside. He climbed off the stool to grab a bulb, then climbed back up to screw it in. Climbed down again to turn on the light switch, and let out another relieved sigh when the new bulb glowed bright. Perfect. No spending money he didn't have. No making Ginsberg more comfortable.

He was halfway through replacing the second bulb when he heard water running in the bathroom. Just a trickle—the sink, then. Not the shower. Which explained the lack of noise coming from Ginsberg's room. He climbed up the stool with the second bulb, then climbed down when he was done screwing it in.

Just then the bathroom door opened, and a *very not dressed* Ginsberg took two steps, saw Derrick, and froze like a startled rabbit.

"Uh." Ever so slowly, he clutched at the too-small towel slung low on his waist, too late for Derrick to miss the peek of dark hair trailing down from his navel.

"Uh," Derrick parroted back, feeling about as stunned as Ginsberg looked.

But then the moment seemed to pass—for Ginsberg, anyway. He smiled, all the tension draining from his posture and expression, and said, not worried exactly but clearly *exploratory*, "Guess I should've brought a spare change of clothes in with me, huh?"

"Uh," Derrick said again, because his mind was still way too busy processing the fact that he was suddenly rock fucking hard for a rooster-head city boy. And he was standing in a dim hallway clutching a lightbulb like an idiot while his unwanted guest was grinning at him without shame, with . . . was that *amusement*?

And sure, why not amusement? Because Derrick's eyes kept trying to politely slide off of Ginsberg's body but somehow kept sliding back onto it instead, and though he knew he was licking his lips he couldn't stop himself, and what the hell did Ginsberg have to be ashamed *of* anyway? His body was enviously hard and lean, muscles glistening and small dark nipples peaked after the shower he must've taken. Writhing, monochromatic tattoos covered his smooth skin from his collarbones down to his hands—or what Derrick could see of it, anyway, around the cast going palm to elbow. Derrick studied the tattoos for a moment before his gaze was drawn to the deep brown, half-curled hair that trailed from Ginsberg's navel to the edge of his towel. Not even the strangely familiar twin scars seamed down either side of his chest detracted from how *hot* he was. And *definitely* not his cocky, confident smile as he watched Derrick uselessly trying to get himself back together.

"You need something?" Ginsberg finally asked.

"No! I'll— I'll just—" Derrick waved helplessly toward the stairs.

"I didn't say you had to *go*." Ginsberg's dark eyes twinkled. "Just . . . avert your eyes."

Derrick did him one better: he clapped a palm right over both of them.

He heard Ginsberg's laugh, then the sound of him unlocking his bedroom door and padding inside.

A couple minutes later, the door closed again. "Okay, I'm decent," Ginsberg said, and when Derrick lowered his hand, Ginsberg was standing in front of him again, but now he had on a pair of jeans, his T-shirt tossed over one shoulder.

"Like my scars?" Ginsberg asked, gesturing to his chest, which Derrick *thought* he hadn't been staring at too obviously, but apparently not. "Pretty badass, right? Definitely more badass than this gross burn." He half turned, showing off a shiny web of skin over his shoulder blade. "Although with the burn scar, I got paid leave. Not so much with the other two. *Man*, it sucked having to take that much time off work."

"What failing B&B did you wind up in that time?" Derrick asked. He'd meant it as a joke, but his mouth still felt completely disconnected from his brain, so it didn't come out sounding funny at all.

"B&B?" Ginsberg faked an uproarious laugh. "What, you think I've always lived this good? No way. Back then I had to suck it up and stay in a youth hostel. Well, that and a couple weeks on my ex-girlfriend's couch because even with a bit of bad blood between us at the time, she still couldn't stand the thought of me recovering from major surgery in a room I was sharing with a couple of crusty Germans." He curled his nose. "In hindsight, she was probably right. I'm lucky I didn't get some terrible infection."

Youth hostels? His ex-girlfriend's couch? What about an apartment somewhere? Or his parents' place? *Any* relative's, come to think of it. Was he all by himself? Derrick's resolve to just tell the guy to leave so he could close up shop like he'd planned wavered slightly.

"Yeah, uh." He took in the dim hallway, walls desperate for a coat of paint, carpet thin, everything coated in a layer of dust. "Can't promise you won't get some terrible infection here, either."

But Ginsberg just laughed, like Derrick was making a joke rather than a warning.

"I uh." He pointed to the stairwell with the lightbulb in his hand. Two fresh bulbs out of three would have to do now: enough light to prevent an accident, enough dimness to feel grim. "I'll leave you to it." Whatever *it* was. Standing around looking way too hot for comfort, maybe. Or maybe being more comfortable in his skin than Derrick was. "Got things to do today, so you're on your own. Better get an early night if you want a hot breakfast tomorrow, though. I don't sleep in, and I don't cater to people who do. I expect you downstairs at 6 a.m."

If the lack of sunlight and fluffy bedding and hot water didn't make Ginsberg check out soon, then hopefully an ass-crack of dawn wake-up call would. Kids these days were anything *but* early risers.

Ginsberg probably rolled out of bed past noon, and stayed up well into the night. If that turned out to be the case, Derrick would have to make sure the after-hours noise rules were extra strictly enforced.

Maybe he wouldn't have to tell Ginsberg to leave after all. Not like Derrick wasn't a natural at being a shitty host. Even if he realized, as he gathered up his tools and step stool and headed down the stairs, that he was feeling pretty guilty at just the thought of doing bad on *purpose*.

But really, Ginsberg would be better off somewhere else. Somewhere with his own kind, who blow-dried their ridiculous haircuts and made stupid TV shows and didn't wake up at the crack of dawn to chop wood. People who weren't trying to run from their failures and their dead parents' hopes and dreams.

For both their sakes, Ginsberg had to go.

Fortunately, Derrick had driven off plenty of guests in his time running the B&B, and that had been when he was trying to get them to stick around. He'd already been a jerk about breakfast, and room choices, and accidentally staring at Ginsberg's half-naked body for at least a minute solid. The next step was easy: the one thing he *never* did when he actually wanted his guests to stay for their entire reservation. The one thing even a fuckup like Derrick had known would be kryptonite for his parents' business.

Bring his mother's dog home.

So while Ginsberg got the rest of the way dressed upstairs, Derrick grabbed the cordless phone in the sitting room to call up his dog sitter. Who was also, as it happened, his ex, an aging twink named Jim who Derrick had enjoyed regular weekend booty calls with all the way from their junior year of high school through to just a couple years ago. He'd always been way too theatrical and queeny for Derrick's dating tastes—not that Derrick ever dated—but he'd been a staunchly loyal friend, even against all those asshole school bullies (*Do you two queens share a room at the Bayview?*), and he'd proven himself boyfriend material while helping Derrick pick up the pieces after his parents' death. When the grief had eased up enough for Derrick to stop being so shamelessly clingy, though, it'd quickly become obvious to both of them that Jim was boyfriend material for *somebody else*.

But as much as Derrick wanted a clean break from the guy and to put the past in the past, Jim's brief time as Derrick's One and Only also meant he was also the only person in the world who could tolerate Derrick's mother's hateful Yorkshire terrier, Victoria. Which didn't mean Victoria liked him—far from it, the dog absolutely despised him. But Jim loved Victoria. He probably also loved the fact that Victoria gave him an excuse to remain useful to—and therefore stay in touch with—Derrick.

He dialed, and Jim answered with a cheerful "Yello!" on the second ring.

"Hey, Jim."

"Dicky-doo!" Jim squealed. "Wasn't expecting a call from you until Friday. What can I do you for?"

Derrick cleared his throat, flinching at the horrible pet name. "Uh, well, that's the thing. I can actually come get Victoria early."

"Oh no." He could just *hear* Jim's exaggerated pout. "Dicky, Dicky, Dicky. What did you do this time?"

"Probably a combination of things, but I doubt setting the kitchen on fire cooking breakfast helped."

"On fire? Holy shit, are you okay? You didn't burn the house down, did you?"

"Luckily, no. The new guy I got staying here was pretty good with a fire extinguisher and put it all out. Now I just have to clean up the mess."

"You already have a new guest?" Jim asked. "I thought you said you were ready to take Victoria back?"

"Oh, I am." That came out sounding slightly ominous, so Derrick coughed and added, "New guy's long-term, so I didn't want to leave Victoria with you all that time." Another pause while he scrabbled for an excuse or explanation Jim would accept without asking too many questions. "I talked it over with him and he says he's fine with it. He *loves* dogs."

"Well, she's your dog and it's your decision, but can I just say, as someone who cares about you—"

"Nope. You can't say anything. Especially not if you're prefacing it with that gushy love talk. You want me to pick her up, or do you want to drop her off?"

"Oh, drop her off, definitely. I have *got* to see how 'fine with it' this guy is once he meets her."

Derrick cast a look at the ceiling, where he could hear Ginsberg's footfalls on the squeaky old floorboards two stories up. "I don't know if you'll get to meet him. I'm sure he's just gonna want to stick to himself and get settled since it's his first day n'all."

"I'm willing to take the chance," Jim replied, sounding a hell of a lot like he was smirking.

The old bird always did know him too damn well.

So that happened.

Standing there naked in front of Derrick, there'd been a moment, of course—one single familiar moment—where Ginsberg had feared for his safety. But it had come and gone awfully quick. Sure, Derrick was a big guy (though Ginsberg still would've bet a month's lodging he could take him if not for the stupid cast), and he was a gruff bastard, but he wasn't *mean*. And not entirely straight either, because there was absolutely no denying the way Derrick had been swallowing Ginsberg whole with his eyes. Not that Ginsberg planned to go there with him.

No matter how scruffy-flannel-wrapped-handsome he was.

Was lumberjack-*chic* a thing?

At least he'd been wearing a towel, so he still had a bit of privacy left. But if Derrick had figured out his scars, there were no guarantees he wasn't going to spend the rest of their time together furiously pretending that it'd never happened; Ginsberg had been around more than his fair share of folks who got weird or flustered or awkward or uncomfortable or all of the above after learning he was trans.

Well, as ever, there was only one way to find out. Just because he had no intention of falling into bed with a guy who'd clearly been raised by the local wolf population—and maybe Derrick had no intention of falling into bed with *him,* either—that didn't mean they couldn't be social. Much as Ginsberg wasn't looking forward to how their next meeting might go (*please don't be awkward please don't be awkward please don't be awkward*), there was no way he'd be spending the next eight to twelve weeks it'd take for his arm to heal hiding in his tomb-like little room. He needed to stay active. Stay out there. Not being on set every day—with actors and PAs and makeup artists and craft-service workers all around—was going to *suck*, and getting lonely and depressed would in no way help his healing.

The degree to which his forced exile would suck, though, wasn't entirely up to him. But until Hot and Grumpy proved otherwise, Ginsberg was choosing to believe their nearly nude encounter had changed nothing. So he put on his dry shirt, locked his bedroom door, and tramped down the stairs to the sitting room with its cozy fire.

Derrick was on the couch, half-asleep in front of the flickering television. He visibly startled when Ginsberg walked into the room.

"Thought you had things to do?" Ginsberg teased, testing the waters further by throwing himself down on the couch next to Derrick.

He felt sorry for saying it, even as a joke, when Derrick sniffed. "I *am* doing things. Watching TV is doing a thing."

So he *was* going to be weird, then. Ginsberg's chest tightened, but he stayed put. "Fair enough." He shrugged, trying to defuse the tension. "Whatcha watching?"

"Some misery auction show. You know, bunch of asshole reality TV types all bid on some bankrupt dead person's abandoned belongings for profit."

Huh. Maybe not so weird? "Ugh." Ginsberg scrunched his nose. "Just when I thought reality TV couldn't get any more horrible."

Derrick made no attempt to reply, but that was fine by Ginsberg. There was no uncomfortable silence in the world that a good rant couldn't fill.

"Cheap-ass TV producers looking to make a quick buck for the least amount of investment cut out a bunch of jobs—including mine—from their productions, which, by the way, are staged as hell anyhow. Every one of these shows gets more and more outrageous and exploitative in an attempt to compete in an already saturated market."

"Whoa now, son." Derrick looked at him askance, eyebrows lifted. "Don't hold back, tell us how you *really* feel."

"Sorry," Ginsberg said with a sheepish laugh.

On second glance, though, that eyebrow lift of Derrick's seemed less judgmental or disbelieving than it was helplessly charmed.

So . . . no weirdness after all, then? Could he *be* that lucky?

"Don't be," Derrick said. "Losing your job because the industry's changing . . . I get that. Trust me."

"Forestry, right?" Ginsberg watched him out of the corner of one eye, for some reason too shy all of a sudden to turn and face him properly. "That must be tough."

Derrick stared at the television. Grunted. Ginsberg started to think he would have to take the reins of their conversation again, but then Derrick spoke. "What about you? What job do you do down on *Wolf's Landing* that you can't do in reality TV? They don't need people who do the clothes on reality TV? That can't be right. Somebody gotta pick out them camouflage suits they wear on *Duck Dynasty*."

Ginsberg smothered a grimace. God, what if he was one of those gay panic closeted types, looking at him like meat then turning around to beat the shit out of him on a dime? "What makes you think I do costume design?"

Now it was Derrick's turn to look sheepish. "I don't know. Your hair and your clothes and all that, I guess."

Okay, so maybe closet-case homophobe was a little premature. Maybe just effemiphobic. Not so surprising in the timber trade, and Ginsberg could work with it. "I'm going to take that as a compliment," he told Derrick pointedly. "But no, I don't do costumes. Or makeup, before you suggest that. I'm a stunt performer."

"A . . . What?"

"Have you seen *Wolf's Landing* at all?"

Derrick shook his head.

Too bad Ginsberg wasn't really comfortable enough with Derrick to talk about any of his female roles, because he'd done some pretty awesome, gory stunts on B-horror sets before he'd transitioned. Post-transition, he had plenty of dumb action movies under his belt, but the problem with those was that with so many big set pieces, it was hard for any of them to be truly memorable. So he defaulted to the biggest blockbuster he'd been in. He could work his way down from there. "How about *Dead at Dawn*?"

Derrick perked up. "Oh! Yeah, I saw that one. Not in 3D though. I hate that stuff."

"Okay. Well, remember the scene where Romero corners that waiter at the Chinese restaurant because he knows the villain does business there? And the waiter gets spooked and tries to rabbit, but then the villain's there too, and it looks like there's gonna be a shoot-out, but then the waiter just starts throwing live seafood out of the restaurant's tank?"

That got a laugh. "I do! And he tosses a fuckin' king crab and Romero shoots it in midair like a skeet!"

"Right!" Ginsberg said, a laugh bubbling up in him, too. "Well, the crabs and lobsters being thrown were just props, but they filmed the scene with live seafood in the tank. They all had elastic bands on their pincers and everything, but the actor still didn't want to stick his hand in the tank—or maybe it was the higher-ups saying he couldn't because he didn't have insurance for that kind of thing—so whatever, long story short is that was actually me doing the bits where the waiter dunks his hand. And let me tell you, pincers or no pincers, those fuckers' shells are pretty goddamn sharp. And it was a saltwater tank, so it burned like a bitch the whole time."

"I had no idea," Derrick said, leaning forward, eyes locked on Ginsberg's. "I figured they just did all that with computer animation nowadays."

"Computer animation's expensive, man. It's still cheaper to let crazy shits like me give it a go." He grinned.

"What else you done? Anything I've seen? Is that how you broke your arm?"

Ginsberg practically bounced in his seat at discovering how to crack Derrick's crusty exterior. His mind raced through his movies, trying to find something similarly violent and badass and absurd to impress him with, but then the doorbell rang.

CHAPTER FOUR

Goddamn it! Derrick couldn't believe it, but he was actually regretting asking Jim to bring the dog home. Ginsberg was proving to be far less of a big-city nancy boy than Derrick had first assumed, and there were so many things Derrick found himself wanting to ask. About his other stunt jobs. About how he'd broken his arm. About working with various actors and actresses. About if he had any *other* interesting scars that maybe Derrick hadn't seen in that upstairs hallway.

And instead, he was flashing an apologetic smile as the doorbell rang for the *third fucking time*.

"I'm coming!" he roared over the doorbell's fourth ring, getting up to answer the damn thing.

He opened the door a fraction.

"Dick!" Jim squealed. Victoria let out a peal of barks.

Derrick extended his arms, flinching in expectation as he did so.

"Aw, can't I at least come in?" Jim hugged Victoria closer, making it clear he didn't intend to hand her over unless he got his invitation. Victoria growled and yipped and squirmed in his arms, little nails clawing at his chest.

"Really not a good time," he said through his teeth. He most definitely didn't want Jim meeting Ginsberg. Not now, not ever. The two of them together, chatterbugs that they both were, would no doubt gossip him to death.

Jim scowled and sniffed. "You're no fun. Well, see if I dog-sit for *you* again!" He pushed Victoria against Derrick's chest in a huff, and stormed off down the drive to where his silver Prius was parked.

He'd be back. He loved to make a show of being offended by Derrick's multitudes of slights and wrongdoings, but he always came back in the end.

In the meantime—

"Fuck!" Derrick yelped as Victoria's tiny terrier teeth sank into the fleshy base of his thumb. Lightly, not enough to draw blood, but he still dropped her in surprise.

She scurried down the hall, yapping and nails scrabbling, heading straight for the living room.

A moment later, Ginsberg let out a bloodcurdling scream.

Derrick, feeling guilty even though everything was clearly going according to plan, made a run for it.

When he burst into the room, Ginsberg was standing on the couch, face contorted in exaggerated fear, while Victoria hopped around on the floor at his feet, barking and growling but too small to reach him.

Derrick leaned against the doorframe and smirked. "So you work a job where you have to put your hand into tanks of king crabs and probably get lit on fire and jump off of buildings and shit, but you're scared of a little dog?"

"That is *not* a dog!" Ginsberg exclaimed, and with his flair for drama, it was no wonder he was on TV. "It's a rat! A lab experiment gone wrong! A furry demon! A chupacabra!"

Derrick cracked a smile. "*She* is a Yorkshire terrier. Her *name* is Victoria Beckham."

Ginsberg stopped squealing. "Her . . . name . . ." he echoed, and Derrick could see the exact moment of recognition. "Victoria Beckham," he said to himself, and snorted, and then began to laugh. He hopped down from the couch, and crouched to Victoria's level as she jumped from side to side, still yapping away. "I can see the resemblance," he said, and actually reached out to pat Victoria's tiny vicious head with the curled, casted fingers of his bad arm. Victoria took a leap and bit into his cast, then fell to the floor, stunned.

Then she rushed forward, took a cautious sniff at Ginsberg's still-extended hand, and *licked his fingers*.

Derrick gaped at them both. "My, uh . . ." He blinked as Ginsberg scooped Victoria up with his good arm and settled back onto the sofa again with her in his lap. She circled twice, then lay down, her beady eyes half-closed in either bliss or suspicion. "My mother named her."

Still scratching behind Victoria's ears, Ginsberg chuckled. "I thought maybe a woman had a hand in that. Or an effeminate man, possibly. Who *was* the guy at the door, anyway?"

Gulp. Well, worst-case scenario, Ginsberg would turn out to be an unlikely homophobe, and if so, he'd surely move out. Which was what Derrick was aiming for here, wasn't it? Besides, he couldn't imagine what kind of mental acrobatics Ginsberg would've had to do to interpret Derrick's behavior in the hallway earlier today as anything but sexual interest. Curiosity, sure, but curiosity didn't make a guy lick his lips while he was staring. So he was pretty sure Ginsberg was safe to tell. "He's my ex."

Ginsberg nodded once, but didn't otherwise react. Derrick wasn't sure whether he was relieved by that or disappointed. "Are you *sure* he didn't name the dog?"

"Nah. That was my mom."

"Oh! So it's her dog, then?"

The air in Derrick's lungs froze. "*Was*," he corrected, hoping Ginsberg would let the matter lie.

He did, although there was no mistaking the pity on his face. Well, let him jump to conclusions if he wanted to. Derrick wouldn't spill any more details. Hadn't spilled any details at all, really. He could have just adopted Victoria after his parents moved to Australia or something. Or maybe their theoretical nursing home didn't allow pets. Plenty of possibilities other than the sob story of them being dead.

"Did she name you 'Dick,' too?" Ginsberg asked at last, his eyes twinkling with mischief. His expression, and the fact that he had Victoria settled in his lap, made him look like a hipster Bond villain.

"She didn't *name* me Dick," Derrick spat. "She named me Derrick." He sighed, and added in a mumble, "She just called me Dick as a nickname."

Ginsberg spluttered.

Derrick's mouth pressed into a line. "Yeah, yeah, get it out of your system. My mom's nickname for me was—"

"Dick and Vick!" Ginsberg chortled. "You rhyme! That's so cute!"

"... a slang word for penis," Derrick finished, too surprised to stop himself. He bristled. "And hey, like you can talk! The fuck kind of name is *Ginsberg*, anyway? Giiinsberg."

Ginsberg pursed his lips. "Ah, yes, *that*." He thought the matter over a moment, then said carefully, "Well, I happen to have had the unusual opportunity to pick my own name." His lazy mouth twisted into half a smile. "Sadly, that opportunity came in my early twenties when I was all rebellious and angry and queer. Thus, Ginsberg."

That explanation . . . raised more questions than it answered, actually. Derrick gave him a blank look.

"After Allen Ginsberg?"

Derrick shook his head.

"Poet? Gay? Influential part of the Beat movement? James Franco played him in a half-shitty-half-amazing biopic? No?"

Again, Derrick shook his head.

"Man, Ginsberg's poetry got me through some tough times growing up queer. Did you have something like that?"

Derrick scoffed like the very concept was absurd. Then he changed the subject. "What do you mean, you had the opportunity to pick your name? How come? Your parents saddle you with a stupid one? Stupider than Ginsberg, that is?"

Ginsberg's mouth twisted. His hand moved a little more rapidly through Victoria's fur. He paused. Put back his shoulders. "You could kind of say that. Well, no, it wasn't *inherently* stupid, but it was all wrong for me. It was . . . a girl's name." He went silent then, staring right into Derrick's eyes like he'd just dropped a bombshell.

Ohhh. "So I'm guessing," Derrick said delicately, "by the way you're looking at me, it wasn't like that song 'A Boy Named Sue'?"

"I'm transgender," Ginsberg said, calm and clear.

Suddenly, Derrick remembered where he'd last seen scars like the ones on Ginsberg's chest: on Jim's friend Aiden, who'd introduced himself as, "FTM, do you have a fucking problem with that?"

Suddenly, too, Ginsberg's lack of family, lack of a home to return to, made horrible sense as well. Someone somewhere had abandoned him, kicked him out, left him in the rain for being who he was, the same way Derrick had always feared his father might do to him if he ever learned the truth.

There was no way in hell Derrick could tell him he had to leave now. Because dollars to donuts, more than one person the kid had loved and trusted had told him the same thing. And after a life like that, could Derrick blame Ginsberg if he thought Derrick was kicking him out because he was queer?

Even if Ginsberg *didn't* jump to that obvious conclusion, Derrick knew how much it hurt to be rejected. He *couldn't* inflict that kind of pain on this relentlessly optimistic kid.

He also couldn't keep on like this, limping along and ruining his parents' reputation, driving their one-time dream as deep into the ground as their bodies were. Derrick needed to shut the B&B down, and for that Ginsberg needed to go. And if Derrick couldn't in good conscience tell him to find new lodging, then he really would have to . . . convince Ginsberg to leave of his own accord.

As guilty as that made him feel, it was for the best. For the both of them.

"So, um . . ." Ginsberg's tentative expression, brave but wincing as he awaited Derrick's response, made Derrick's heart pound, made him desperate to make this right, even for just a little while.

"My parents are dead," he blurted out, wanting to offer something in kind. A secret for Ginsberg, who'd trusted Derrick with his own. "This used to be their B&B. And now it's mine."

Ginsberg smiled. The thankfulness in his expression was unmistakable, even to a guy like Derrick who was as far from touchy-feely as you could get.

And Derrick, lack of touchy-feelyness be damned, smiled right back.

They had a hell of a time getting conversation started up again after their respective revelations. While Ginsberg didn't mind that one bit, Derrick seemed increasingly uncomfortable, so Ginsberg cut him some slack, tactfully suggesting that maybe Derrick could let him dog-sit while he went into town for a new fire extinguisher.

Derrick jumped at the offer to get out of there, adding, "Better get some dog food, too."

Ginsberg, sprawled on the couch with the TV on and Victoria Beckham curled up on his chest, cheerfully waved Derrick off, but as soon as the front door shut, he leapt to his feet.

Victoria Beckham yelped and yapped, running around his ankles in confused circles. Ginsberg ignored her, floating into the smoke-clouded kitchen on a pink breeze of warm and gooey feelings.

There'd been no weirdness. There'd been, in fact, the exact *opposite* of weirdness.

Sure, he'd been lucky enough to have had guys—even manly man lumberjack types like Derrick—react with tact and empathy to discovering that he was trans before, but there was something special about the way Derrick's gruff demeanor had softened just for him. And not in a condescending way, either. The guy obviously had a secret sensitive side, and Ginsberg was *into it*.

And he seriously needed to get himself together, because hadn't he decided ages back not to put too much weight into shows of basic human decency? Sure, it was nice (and safe, one could never overlook the importance of safe) that Derrick was so accepting, but it didn't mean he deserved a medal or anything.

Well . . . maybe he *did* deserve a medal for toiling against all odds to keep his parents' dream alive when they weren't. Plenty of guys in Derrick's position would have closed up shop, sold the place for a quick buck, and moved on. Derrick, despite clearly not having a single hospitality bone in his body, was still here. Setting his kitchen on fire and getting blasted all over the internet, but still here. He wasn't an heir to a big successful business, carrying on a legacy. The Bayview B&B was a labor of love. And Ginsberg had love to spare.

He cranked the kitchen window over the sink wide open. Turned on the fan above the stove. Used a tea towel one-handed to flap some of the fumes out the window, just for good measure.

There was an old transistor radio on top of the fridge, and Ginsberg twisted the dials until he found a fuzzy but still-serviceable college radio broadcast playing upbeat indie music to work to.

It looked like Derrick had made a halfhearted attempt to clean up the powder from the fire extinguisher, but it also looked like he'd given up thirty seconds in. Ginsberg found a few scant cleaning supplies in the cupboard under the sink: a scummy bottle of Windex, some no-name dish soap, and a lone ball of steel wool. Not even a sponge to his name—or at least, not one Ginsberg felt safe using. The one by the sink went straight into the trash can, hopefully taking all its soggy bacteria with it.

Luckily, the guy did have baking soda and vinegar in a different cupboard, so Ginsberg was able to get his Pinterest on.

He got the blackened "food" into the trash can, then filled the various charred pans with baking soda and vinegar. He washed dishes. Cleaned the oven. Wiped down the stove top. Cleaned out the fridge.

Being a seasoned "considerate couchsurfer"—as Ginsberg liked to refer to himself—he had lots of practice with cleaning other peoples' kitchens and cooking "thank you for not putting me on the street" meals. Derrick didn't exactly have a well-stocked kitchen, but Ginsberg was used to that, too. It seemed like the people most willing to open their home to him were always the ones with the least to share.

That was all right. Give him a bag of lentils, some root vegetables, and a spice rack, and he could cobble together a damn edible meal. No lentils in roughneck Derrick's kitchen, but Ginsberg did find a couple of fat steaks in a styrofoam tray on the top shelf of his fridge. The guy also had a few—growing, but still usable—potatoes under his sink. Ginsberg could make this work. Make a nice peppercorn sauce, roast the potatoes up crispy, sear the steaks medium rare. All that was missing was some mushrooms.

Oh, but Derrick did have a yellow onion stuck in with his potatoes. And a few bottles of beer. And oil for frying. Beer-battered onion rings it was.

A lunch fit for kings. Or maybe an early dinner, as the case may be. It was nearly four now—he'd been enjoying Derrick's company (and nice warm fire) so much he hadn't even noticed skipping lunch—and he still had a lot of cooking in front of him. He'd probably wind up walking around with a food-baby potbelly for two days after this, but hey, not like he had to do any strenuous runs, jumps, fights, or falls anytime soon.

He did do a bit of one-armed dancing to The Strokes while he picked eyes off of the potatoes and started dicing them for the roasting pan. Which was easier said than done with one arm in a cast, not surprisingly. Using his good arm to handle the knife, he attempted to keep the potatoes steady with his casted hand while he cut. They shot out of his half-immobilized fingers and off the counter more than once, Victoria Beckham chasing them across the kitchen floor while barking blue murder.

Soon the kitchen was full of the smells of onion and meat and beer, and full of the sounds of sizzling oil and Modest Mouse and Victoria Beckham's yaps and sneezes as she danced around Ginsberg's feet for attention and/or scraps.

He was dipping his onion rings in the batter when he heard the front door open and heavy workman's boots tromping down the hall. He dropped his last onion in the oil, wiped his batter-hand on a towel, and turned.

"The hell?" Derrick asked, standing in the doorway and giving his leg a shake as Victoria Beckham tried her damnedest to scale it.

Was he surprised? Was this what a grumpy guy like Derrick looked like when he was surprised?

Or was he just pissed?

Ginsberg decided to give him the benefit of the doubt, but he still found himself smiling and shrugging. "You seemed like you were having a shitty day. I figured a home-cooked meal couldn't hurt."

Derrick sniffed suspiciously. "Is that . . . steak?"

"And onion rings," Ginsberg offered, feeling as needy as a puppy. As needy as Victoria Beckham, to be specific. Derrick hadn't bent down to greet her yet, and she was going fucking crazy.

"Smells good," Derrick finally said, and Ginsberg sagged with relief.

"Well it'll be ready in a few more minutes, so how about you get a table set for us?" Ginsberg turned back to the stove, but didn't stop himself casting a cheeky smile over his shoulder. "And in the meantime, pick up your poor dog, would you? You're torturing her."

"You think this is her wanting to be picked up?" Derrick scoffed, then crouched, hand extended.

Victoria Beckham barked and snapped and growled, hopping in a semicircle back and forth in front of Derrick a few times before retreating to a more fortified position behind Ginsberg's legs.

Hiding from her owner behind *him*?

He gaped at Derrick, who just shrugged before making a beeline to a corner cupboard for the plates. "I don't know how you did it," he said, giving his head a little shake. "But you did."

Somehow, Ginsberg got the impression he wasn't talking just about winning Victoria Beckham over.

CHAPTER FIVE

It didn't take Derrick long to remember why Ginsberg had to go. Talking poets with him? Cooking for him? What were they, high school sweethearts? And shit, shouldn't a guy like Ginsberg be a little more careful about doing girly stuff like this if he wanted to be accepted as a man?

The kid needed to get his priorities straight.

And so did Derrick. As charming as Ginsberg could be, Derrick had already decided to close this place down. That was it. Final. He was done stomping his parents' legacy into the dirt. He was done trying to be anything but the simple loner of a man he was. Maybe Ginsberg could play fast and loose with the rules that divided men and women—if they even applied to him in the first place—but Derrick wasn't like that. Bayview B&B needed to close its doors so that Derrick could get back to the real world.

And for that, Ginsberg needed to move out.

Yet for some reason, he obediently set them a table in the breakfast room.

The plates from this morning's disastrous breakfast were still sitting on one of the other tables, and when Ginsberg showed up with their meal, Victoria Beckham trailing merrily behind him, there was no missing that they'd caught his attention. A puppy dog look of pity settled across his young, unguarded face.

Anything but pity. Derrick could live with condemnation, but not pity. This place had unmanned him enough already.

At least Ginsberg didn't comment.

But it didn't make Derrick any more comfortable with Ginsberg's expression. He snorted at the plate put in front of him, even though it looked damn good and his stomach was growling from a missed lunch. "Don't think that just because you're making yourself useful I'm gonna give you a discount on your rate," he grumbled.

"Being useful's its own reward," Ginsberg replied. He cast Derrick a friendly smile, as if he'd been complimented.

Derrick couldn't stand to look at him right now, so he stared more resolutely at his plate.

Which wasn't much better for his ego, because the food Ginsberg had prepared really seemed amazing. The steak was dark and crusted with seasoning, and the onion rings were crispy and fat. There was even some kind of sauce. Derrick would have just fried this steak up and eaten it in a puddle of store-bought barbecue sauce with premade french fries on the side. And as much as he had tried to twist Ginsberg's cooking into a slight against his masculinity, there was no denying that it was a pretty manly meal. All it needed was— "You want a beer, kid?"

Ginsberg's expression was best described as *kid on Christmas*. "Please!"

Derrick's face heated as he stood. If he was trying to drive Ginsberg out, he was doing a bang-up job of it. With a grunt of acknowledgment, he escaped to the kitchen, then came back with two opened bottles in hand. He set one wordlessly in front of Ginsberg, and then sat down with his own.

Ginsberg was still giving him that same dopey smile as he took a swig.

"Are you even old enough to be drinking this?" he asked irritably.

He'd meant it as a jab, but Ginsberg just smirked at him, seemingly pleased as ever. "How old do you think I am?" he asked, sipping smugly at his beer without ever taking his eyes off Derrick.

Derrick shrugged. This was not the intended result of his question. This was . . . conversation. Getting to know each other. Possibly even flirting, judging by the smarmy fucking smile on Ginsberg's face. He wasn't supposed to be doing any of those things. And yet, he was helpless but to play along. "I dunno, too young for beer."

"Go on, guess!" Ginsberg propped his chin on his good hand.

Little shit. Derrick leaned back in his seat, prodding at his potatoes with his fork. "I dunno," he said, again, resisting the urge to squirm. "C'mon, you're making me feel like an idiot."

Ginsberg's expression softened. He sat back, all the smug teasing draining away. "I'm thirty-one."

"Get out of town," Derrick replied. "Get the fuck out."

Ginsberg chuckled and took another sip of his beer. Dug into his potatoes. "It's true. I still get carded."

"You *are* pretty short." Derrick flinched as soon as he said it. Maybe that wasn't the sort of thing you joked about with someone like Ginsberg. He could just hear some asshole tacking on *like a woman* at the end. Derrick wasn't that asshole, but how was Ginsberg supposed to know that?

But Ginsberg just shrugged. "It's the body I've got."

Derrick couldn't help his curiosity. "Is that how you feel about . . . all of it?"

His question earned him a raised eyebrow. "That's pretty heavy for a first date, Mr. Richards."

"Sorry, sorry," Derrick sputtered, but Ginsberg laughed.

"It's fine, dude. I'm just fucking with you. I'll cut you slack since at least you didn't ask me about my plumbing. But yeah, that's how I feel about *all of it*. Took me a while to get there, but . . ."

"You had Allen Ginsberg?" Derrick tried.

"*And* nonbook friends; I'm not a total loser." Ginsberg smiled. "What about you? How was it for you, growing up queer?"

"If you're looking to commiserate over a sob story, keep walkin', kid." But despite himself, Derrick cleared his throat, strangely compelled. "My ma knew. I think the kids at school knew, too. Called me all sorts of names, but maybe that was just because I worked the B&B. Girls' work, you know . . ." But apparently Ginsberg didn't know; his expression slipped toward a scowl, and Derrick hastened to explain. "They, uh, called me a maid, teased me about feather dusters and laundry and little black dresses and all that. I never dated anyone in high school, never said anything, but . . . I think they knew. My dad didn't, though. I don't think he'd have disowned me or nothing, but I didn't want to disappoint him, either. You know? He was proud of the man he raised. I wasn't gonna ruin that."

Ginsberg looked sad. "Even if you did come out, I don't think you could have ruined it."

This from the vain city kid, Derrick scoffed inwardly. Hardly the best judge of character when it came to affairs of manhood.

He didn't say any of that, though. Seemed cruel.

But maybe he should have said *something*, because when he didn't, Ginsberg reached across the table and clasped Derrick's fist in his own smaller hand.

Derrick pulled back. "Don't get all touchy-feely on me," he groused.

Ginsberg drew away immediately, the gesture respectful. "Sorry. Despite the badass day-to-day of my job, I'm still an artist. Touchy-feely's part and parcel." His eyes twinkled.

"Is your sense of fashion part and parcel, too?"

"Har-har." Ginsberg gave Derrick a once-over. "You're gonna feel sorry for insulting my fashion sense when I come down tomorrow morning wearing a plaid shirt that's pretty much identical to the one you've got on now."

"More like you're gonna feel like a damn idiot when you find out I probably paid a third of the price you did."

"Touché."

Derrick crunched an onion ring. He shouldn't have been enjoying this meal so much—or rather the company, considering their rocky start—yet they were barely eating for all the talking and teasing they were doing. Kept doing, for almost an hour. The last few bites of Derrick's meal were ice cold.

And sure, he'd completely fucked up on the driving-Ginsberg-out front, but even Derrick wasn't enough of a sour puckered asshole to mess with a guy after he'd cleaned his kitchen and cooked for him.

This was a temporary truce, that was all. Like the Christmas soccer game they had in No Man's Land in World War I. As soon as they got up from the table, the battle of the B&B would resume.

Damn though, why did Ginsberg have to be so aggressively *nice*?

Derrick had been planning to resume the battle by not thanking Ginsberg for the food he'd just cooked, but the minute they pushed their plates away, it just fell right out of his mouth: "I haven't had a meal that good in years. Thanks."

The smile he got in reply was physically painful for him to witness. He had to put an end to it.

Too bad he was too much of a damn coward to try.

If he were really dedicated to this whole enterprise, he'd have asked Ginsberg to clean up, but he couldn't shake the thought of what his mother would think. Even with kitchen duties being "women's work" to most of the men in the world, his father still washed up when she cooked. Doing your fair share, that was part of being a man too.

So Derrick did the dishes.

But at least after having done the dishes like a chump, his next chance to screw with Ginsberg wasn't long in coming.

Derrick was sitting in his mother's old office, trying to make heads or tails of the stacks of bills he'd been letting build up, when Ginsberg poked his head through the half-opened door.

"So uh, hey, question, but do you have a washing machine and dryer? I didn't get to wash my stuff before I left my old place. It's okay if you don't—I can just head down to town and use the laundromat, but since I'm not working n'all, a penny saved is a penny earned."

"Sure, kid," Derrick said, got up from his mother's desk, and showed him the way to the laundry room, which was piled with balled-up dirty and clean sheets. Ginsberg didn't say anything about the mess, just thanked Derrick and trotted to his room for his clothes.

An hour or so later, Derrick stopped the dryer midspin, dragged Ginsberg's sopping laundry out, and carried the heavy basket up to the third floor, where he unceremoniously plopped it in front of Ginsberg's room.

"Sorry," he said through the door, making sure to sound not sorry at all. "The dryer's doing that . . . thing it does. I had to take your clothes out. I'll maybe get somebody in to fix the thing next month when my credit cards aren't all tied up."

Ginsberg poked his head out the door. "Next month?" he asked with a flinch.

Derrick shrugged, ignoring the pang of guilt. It was all for the best. For the greater good. Ginsberg would be better off elsewhere, that was a fact, and this place would be better off closed, and it was all gonna happen eventually, so why not help things along?

That's what he told himself, but he couldn't stand the look of disappointment on Ginsberg's face. He fled downstairs.

A few minutes later, he heard the house's front screen door slam.

Off to the laundromat to waste his dwindling money, Derrick hoped/dreaded.

But then he heard a familiar rusty creak in the backyard. He rushed to the back door, and sure enough, there was Ginsberg desperately trying to get his soaking-wet clothes on the line one-handed. Which mostly involved trying to *toss* them over the line, at which point they slithered right off the other side, landing in the still-wet grass while Victoria danced back and forth over them.

Derrick was able to watch this for all of thirty seconds before he couldn't bear it anymore.

"You idiot," he called, stomping into the yard. "They're never going to dry on the line on a day like this. It only just stopped raining, you know that right?"

Ginsberg shrugged, his smile dangerously wobbly.

Don't you dare fucking cry on me, Derrick thought, and that was it. That was it. He started gathering the clothes—the ones fallen in the grass, the ones haphazardly pinned to the line with his mother's rusty old clothespins—and piling them all back in the basket.

"I know, I know. It's ridiculous," Ginsberg babbled, standing by and watching him. "I'm just being cheap. I didn't want to pay for a cab to and from the laundromat *and* have to get quarters for the dryer."

"Forget it," Derrick said. "I'll take care of it."

"You're gonna give me a ride to the laundromat?" Ginsberg asked, sounding vaguely touched.

Well, no, he was gonna put them in his own damn dryer, but on second thought maybe it would be better to go to the laundromat than expose his lie.

"Yeah, kid," he said, defeated. "I'm gonna take you to the laundromat."

CHAPTER SIX

Derrick drove exactly the kind of vehicle Ginsberg expected a guy like him to drive: A shitty rusted-out pickup truck. Manual transmission, naturally. And terrible country music on the radio.

Ginsberg didn't dare complain what with the guy giving him a ride to town and all, but Derrick must have sensed his discomfort or his squirming or the not-so-subtle way he half plugged one ear with his finger—because he snorted and turned off the radio.

Ginsberg let out a relieved sigh. "Thanks for doing this," he said before the topic of the music could get raised. "I know you didn't have to, so I really appreciate it."

"If you didn't have the one arm in a cast, I wouldn't have."

Ginsberg shrugged, grinning. "If you think I'm too proud for your pity, think again."

Derrick barked out one of his rare, half-bitter laughs. Ginsberg couldn't get a grip on those. It certainly wasn't the easy, honest laughs he was used to. Derrick clearly had a lot going on under the surface.

Which, of course, only made a nosy busybody like Ginsberg all the more intrigued.

The guy was obviously stressed. A failing business. Dead parents he still wanted to impress, including a father he'd stayed in the closet for.

He didn't talk much, but what he did say was definitely revealing, and there was no question Ginsberg was falling for it.

As much as Derrick had tried to hide his feelings on the matter, he'd really appreciated that steak. Judging by the contents of his fridge/freezer and the burnt food everywhere else, Ginsberg had a strong hunch the guy didn't eat many nice meals. And judging by the stack of bills and the broken dryer he couldn't afford to fix, he probably didn't get to eat out much, either.

He'd seemed downright relieved to have someone looking after him, honestly.

Well, it wasn't like Ginsberg had a bunch of long painful shifts on set for the foreseeable future, so why not take on a side project?

First order of business: show his gratitude. So as soon as they got to the Bluewater Wash 'N Dry and tossed his clothes in a dryer, he clapped a hand onto Derrick's shoulder. "You mind watching my stuff for a few minutes?"

Derrick shook his head. "Uh, sure? Not like I got anything better to do but sit here."

"Great! Coffee or tea?"

"What?"

"What do you drink, dude? Coffee or tea? I'm gonna run next door to the Stomping Grounds, get us a couple of drinks. I figure I owe you one—it's still cheaper than a cab ride."

Derrick blinked at him, bewildered. That same look he'd given Ginsberg at the mention of his namesake.

"You don't know the Stomping Grounds?"

Derrick shook his head.

"How long have you been living here, again?" Because Ginsberg was pretty sure the sign hanging outside of the Stomping Grounds said *Est. 1997*.

"I don't get out much, I guess," Derrick grumbled, staring at his own lap in that way he did.

"You know, I bet if you got to know other Bluewater Bay business owners, or even just people around town, they could help you. Small towns like this—close-knit communities of *any* makeup—they look out for each other."

"Coffee," Derrick said flatly. "Black."

No point pushing the issue. "Gotcha," Ginsberg said, and left.

He'd been wrong. The Stomping Grounds sign actually said *Est. 1999*. Still plenty of time for Derrick to have stumbled across the place, though.

When he went inside, Tori, the middle-aged former riot grrl goddess who owned the place, was working the counter alongside a barista he'd never seen before: a purple-haired teen with half their head shaved.

Tori gave Ginsberg a friendly wave, then spotted his cast. "Oh my God, baby!" she cried, ducking out from behind the counter. She rushed toward him like a shot, but stopped short, as if worried she might rebreak his wrist. "What the hell happened?"

"It's broken," he replied. "I had to get hit by a car and roll off the windshield, but I landed wrong, and *crack*."

She hissed in sympathy. "How long do you have to wear the cast?"

"Eight to twelve weeks. I'm hoping closer to eight."

"Did they fire you from the production?"

"I'm sure that asshole Finn Larson tried, but they cut me a season contract this year 'cos Carter gets his ass kicked so often they didn't want to risk losing me to another production. My agent tells me it's ironclad, so I'm just on leave for now. Even if Finn probably *is* trying to find a way to weasel out of it and replace me."

She winced. "They still paying you?"

Ginsberg shook his head. "No. But it's not too bad. I've got workers' comp, and a cheap place to stay that includes some meals. I'm not homeless."

She ushered him to the counter, still dripping concern. "What cheap place?" she asked, then added, "And what'll it be?"

"Uh, gimme a large coffee, black, and . . ." He studied the menu. "And a dirty chai latte with almond milk. Large."

She called it to the young barista working next to her.

"How much?" he asked, reaching behind him for his wallet.

"On the house. And what cheap place?"

Ginsberg didn't try to fight her on the free coffee. He knew he couldn't win. He'd just have to tip her real well next time.

"What cheap place, Gins?" Tori repeated.

"Oh my God, don't look at me like that. I'm not living above a meth lab or anything. I'm staying up at the Bayview B&B."

"Ginsberg Sloan! You may not be living above a meth lab, but . . . *that* place? I'm pretty sure they've failed their last couple of health inspections."

"It's not that bad," Ginsberg said, although inwardly he made a note to help Derrick do a deep clean of the kitchen sometime in the next couple of days. "The owner's a really nice guy. You know it was his parents' place, but they died suddenly and now he's running it to keep their dream alive."

"Their dream, the rest of the world's nightmare." Tori put her hands on her skinny hips. "God, I know that look. You're planning on getting your hands dirty with this guy, right? You are *such* a meddler. Don't think everyone in this town doesn't know about you poking around with those two costars of yours."

Ginsberg snorted. "Carter and Levi? You make it sound like I locked them in a room together until they agreed to date. All I did was make a few choice comments. And I wasn't the one who took *the video*, although I sure wish I'd have thought of it! Maybe then I wouldn't have been dying with the will-they-won't-they tension for so long."

Tori shrugged. "All I'm saying is, you need to rest up if you want to get back to your job. Your *real* job. I'm not saying you can't keep busy, but you can't take this B&B onto your shoulders. It's not your responsibility. And neither is the guy who runs it, no matter how starry-eyed you get when you talk about him."

"I do not get *starry-eyed*."

The teen handing Ginsberg his coffee laughed, then pressed their lips together—no, not their, *eir*, according to the name tag Ginsberg could now see. "You kinda do, dude," ey said.

"So who you guys got playing Friday night?" Ginsberg asked, changing the subject. "Is it worth me dragging my poor injured self into town?"

"No," ey said at the same time Tori emphatically answered "Yes!"

They stared at each other, but finally Tori turned to Ginsberg. "Ignore Dean, ey just isn't old enough to have learned to appreciate the subtleties of indie folk. Anyway, we've got this great local four-piece band coming in, call themselves Smiths and Son Canning Co. They do a mix of original stuff and the holy Sufjan Stevens – Iron & Wine – Great Lake Swimmers trifecta."

"*Banjos*," Dean muttered in exaggerated disgust, shaking eir head. "You know I applied here because I thought the boss was gonna be all punk rock?"

"I was punk rock before you were even *born*," Tori snapped back without venom. "One can be punk rock and still understand that the coffeehouse set prefers a certain aesthetic."

"Acoustic singer-songwriter bullshit," Dean said. "Bring on the screamo, I say." Ey gave Ginsberg's outfit and the tattoos peeking from his sleeve an appreciative once-over.

"Hey, don't look at me. I like indie folk as much as the next guy," Ginsberg said with a shrug, and Dean looked visibly sorry.

"W-well," ey sputtered.

"It's okay, bucko. Nothing wrong with having strong opinions. Even if you *are* questioning a grown man's choice of accommodations." He winked in Tori's direction.

"Or the fact that he meddles in his coworkers' love lives," she teased.

"Okay. *Leaving* now." He picked up his cups, which thankfully hadn't cooled too much in all his dawdling. "Thanks again for the free drinks, you two. I'll try and show my face Friday."

"You better!" Tori called, waving him off.

Oh, he planned on it.

And he planned on dragging Derrick along, too.

Their trip to the laundromat had taught Derrick several things: One, that Ginsberg didn't like country music—seemed to find it physically painful, to be precise. Two, that Ginsberg liked fancy coffee drinks enough to go to one of the expensive local cafés. And three, that he wore brightly colored briefs, the sight of which slightly short-circuited the man-centers of Derrick's brain, especially in combination with how generous Ginsberg's ass was.

Two of those facts were relevant to the task at hand. The other was, well . . . the other ended up being plain old-fashioned jerk-off material that night.

Derrick was a bad man and he was going to Hell.

Whether for masturbating to his guest or for carrying out Today's Country Hits warfare, he wasn't sure.

Over the next several days, he kept the TV on the country music video station, even though he thought the videos were obnoxious and insipid. He played the country station on the radio, too. He didn't even really *like* country all that much, but he sure faked it in his efforts to get on Ginsberg's nerves.

Ginsberg never complained, though, and if he was irritated, he didn't show it in any gratifying way. He just left whatever room Derrick and his music were in . . . which unfortunately punished Derrick at least as much as it theoretically punished Ginsberg.

He'd been here for less than a week, and already Derrick was growing accustomed to his company. His optimism. His stories.

On Thursday—Ginsberg's fourth morning at the B&B—determined to override the part of him that wanted to get closer to Ginsberg, Derrick did the unthinkable: he sabotaged Ginsberg's coffee.

He made it with instant granules, watered it down by using only half the suggested amount of coffee per mug, and worst of all, he served decaf.

He also massacred Ginsberg's poor toasted bagel, but that wasn't on purpose.

Dropping the breakfast on the table, he stood by and waited for Ginsberg to complain.

Ginsberg nobly choked down a bite of bagel without comment, but half a sip of coffee was all it took. He slammed the mug down on the table. "Is this instant coffee?" he asked, his voice artificially even.

"Yep," Derrick said. He definitely didn't apologize. "Decaf instant coffee, to be specific."

"Didn't I see an espresso machine in your kitchen?"

"That was my mom's. I have no idea how that damn thing works." Invoking the dead mother; let Ginsberg try to press the issue now.

No dice. Ginsberg was making his excited meddler face—the same one he'd made at dinner that first day—that meant he wasn't letting Derrick off the hook. "You have a manual?"

"I dunno."

"That's fine. I'm sure there's a model number on the machine somewhere. I'll see if I can find some tutorials or instructions or something on the internet."

You have got to be kidding me.

Ginsberg wasn't kidding. He got up right that second and marched into the kitchen. Helpless against the pure force of Ginsberg's personality, Derrick followed.

Other than a quick jog upstairs to get Ginsberg's laptop, neither Ginsberg nor Derrick left the kitchen for quite some time.

CHAPTER SEVEN

"It's not going to work," Derrick complained. With his sleeves rolled up his bulging arms and that expression of intense concentration on his face, it was a little hard for Ginsberg to focus on the coffee.

On the other hand, the whining was making it hard for him to focus on how good Derrick looked, so it kind of balanced out. "It's an espresso, not brain surgery. So can you at least *try* and lay off on the negativity for five minutes?"

Derrick sniffed.

To be fair, Ginsberg understood his frustration. The small kitchen counter was littered with their failed attempts: Burnt espresso. Espresso with escapee grounds floating in it. Watery espresso. Intolerably bitter espresso. There were even soggy espresso grounds all over the floor and walls from when something-they-weren't-sure-what had gone wrong and Derrick had pulled out the portafilter and the espresso grounds had exploded into his face. Victoria Beckham had tried a taste of the floor-grounds, shuddered from head to toe, and skulked to her bed in the corner of the room to lick her paws.

All that, and they hadn't even *attempted* the milk frother yet.

"Don't grind them so fine this time," Ginsberg coached, leaning over Derrick's shoulder. Tongue poking out between his tightly seamed lips, Derrick inserted the portafilter into the grinder with vibrating hands. He adjusted the grinder dial. Pressed the power button with all the gravitas of a man disarming a nuclear bomb.

They both startled when the grinder roared into life. Espresso grounds spewed, covering Derrick's hand in a black dust, but he did manage to get a decent amount of them into the portafilter.

Ginsberg consulted the how-to on his laptop. "Okay, now it says to use your finger—your *clean* finger," he scolded when he spotted Derrick about to dip an unwashed hand into their coffee, "and run it straight across the top so you have a flat surface to work with."

Derrick, after somewhat begrudgingly running his hand under the tap, followed instructions.

Ginsberg handed him the tamper. "This says to exert thirty pounds of pressure."

"Are you shitting me?"

"As ridiculous as it sounds, no I am not. That is what the website says. Damn, I should be tipping my baristas more because this shit is complicated."

"I'm buying one of those Keurig things." Even as he said it, though, he dutifully set the portafilter on the counter and pressed the tamper into it. Was that seriously sweat on his brow?

Not that Ginsberg could talk. He was on fucking tenterhooks just *watching*. "Easy, easy! I think overcompressing them is why they exploded that one time. And c'mon, don't talk like that. Just think how good it'll be for the B&B if you're able to brew gourmet coffee drinks. It'll be a real selling point."

"Oh yeah." Derrick barked out a laugh. "I can see it now. *The breakfast came out burnt black but damn was the coffee good. Thank God I'm from LA and can live on pure caffeine.*"

Ginsberg smiled and snorted. "Just focus on the coffee, okay? One thing at a time."

Done tamping, Derrick held out the portafilter for inspection.

Shit, Ginsberg had no fucking idea what he was even supposed to see. But he smiled encouragingly anyway. "I think you got it, man. Let's give it a go."

Derrick shoved the portafilter into the slot, cranked it sideways, dumped out and rinsed one of their failed espresso cups, set it under the spouts, and turned on the machine.

It grumbled and hissed, and a few seconds later, some promising dribbles made their way into the cup.

"It's working!" Ginsberg squealed. "We did it! We did it!"

Derrick grinned at him, puffing out his chest. The cup filled. The machine turned itself off.

They both leaned in, shoulders knocking together, examining their handiwork.

"Uh . . . Now what?" Derrick asked.

"We drink it, I guess? Make sure it tastes okay?"

"*We*? You do realize this is only one shot, right? You want me to do all this again?"

Well, yes, because Ginsberg hadn't gone through all this to make a single cup of coffee and then have Derrick return to serving nasty instant to his guests.

But maybe the guy deserved to take the rest of the day off.

Wordlessly, Ginsberg went to the cupboard, took out two mugs, and set them down side by side on the counter. He poured half of their espresso shot into each, then used the espresso machine's hot water dispenser to fill both mugs to the top.

He pressed one of the mugs into Derrick's bewildered hands.

"There," he said, self-satisfied. "Americano."

Derrick nervously raised the mug to his lips, drew in a breath through his nose, and took a long sip. His eyes sank closed, and a slow smile spread across his face. Ginsberg had never seen him look so damn relaxed, or even happy, really. The guy looked like he was in Heaven—or had just received an amazing blowjob.

"Good?" Ginsberg asked, smiling too much to take a drink of his own.

There was no trace of Derrick's usual reticence as he slurred out, "Uh-huh."

Well, he couldn't get a better endorsement than that. Ginsberg took a sip of their handiwork.

It wasn't perfect, nowhere near what he could get at the Stomping Grounds, but it was fucking good. He sighed with pleasure, his bones going liquid as the warmth ran through them, and—back against the cupboards—he sank to his ass on the floor.

A few seconds later, Derrick did the same.

Ginsberg was way too blissed out to be surprised. The pair of them sat there, shoulders and thighs brushing, right in their mess of coffee grounds, and drank.

Derrick sat shuffling papers in his office, picking out the most delinquent of the bills he could now actually pay some of with the month's rent Ginsberg had given him. Debating whether he even should or not, because he'd have to give some of the money back if—*no,* when—he got Ginsberg to leave. And he wouldn't have it anymore if he paid this property tax bill. But *could* he get Ginsberg to leave? Because goddamn was that kid a tough nut to crack.

After driving so many guests away while trying his best, Derrick had assumed that it would be easy to send one packing by purposefully doing his worst.

He was wrong.

And given yesterday's fiasco with the coffee, his concern was taking on new urgency.

Because rather than sending Ginsberg packing, that terrible cup of coffee had led to the two of them in close quarters for more than an hour. Solving a problem together. Bickering. Sharing a great cup of coffee. Ginsberg was still here, and not only that, Derrick had discovered he really did like having the kid around. It was hard not to fall for his infectious enthusiasm and can-do attitude. Harder still to resist his sense of humor and his genuine interest in people. He might be a flitty little city boy, but there was no questioning that he cared about getting to know people. Even someone as deliberately hard to get along with as Derrick.

Which made it real damn difficult to screw with the guy. Manipulating someone as honest and giving as Ginsberg made Derrick a prick of the highest order.

Besides, didn't he pride himself on being a fucking man? What kind of *man* snuck around playing stupid damn tricks? If he was any kind of man, he'd sit Ginsberg down and tell him straight up that he wanted to close the business down. Help the guy find a new place to stay. That was the honorable thing to do.

But letting Ginsberg down? Disappointing him? That just made him feel like a failure.

What was worse, this thing with Ginsberg had clearly gone beyond just niceties.

The things Ginsberg said, the way he reacted to Derrick's various fuckups and failures . . . it made him *hope.*

Think about how good it'll be for the B&B.

Ginsberg believed in Derrick. Wanted him to succeed. And even if it was just coffee—and really, what was a cup of coffee in the face of all the other myriad problems with this fucking place?—it felt like it could be something more. Like the first step on a long journey they could make together.

And that was pretty dangerous thinking.

Derrick couldn't afford to hope, any more than he could afford to count on Ginsberg. As well intentioned as the guy was, in a few weeks, he would be gone. Back to his career and his life, and one day, back to LA entirely. So maybe he could help Derrick make a few small changes. Get him feeling optimistic again. But it wouldn't matter, because sooner or later, he'd be gone, and Derrick would be alone.

If Derrick let him, Ginsberg would do nothing but lift him up just to have farther to fall.

And speaking of the guy who seemed destined to drop him from the perpetually gray sky . . .

"Knock knock!" Ginsberg called from the open doorway of Derrick's office instead of *actually* knocking.

Damn it all, but Derrick looked up and smiled. Of *course* he did, and not just because Ginsberg's jeans *and* wifebeater were clinging so tight they might as well have been painted on. Derrick found himself standing up, though he didn't know why. Maybe just to take a step closer to the kid.

Ginsberg's answering grin nearly made Derrick fall back into his seat again. "Sooo, just putting this out there and feel free to say no, but can I maybe be an even bigger imposition on you than I usually am?"

What could Derrick say but, "Anything." Breathlessly. He cleared his throat, avoiding eye contact. "I mean, uh, anything you need, kid."

"I've got a thing in town tonight. At that coffee shop, the Stomping Grounds? Would you maybe go along as my not-date?"

Had Ginsberg really just asked Derrick out? Or, er, not-out? Derrick gaped at him. At his big brown eyes and his teeth worrying at his lower lip and the way he reached across himself with his good hand to clutch at his own upper arm.

He really had.

"It's just . . . if I go on my own I *know* the owner Tori is going to try and teach me a lesson by setting me up with somebody there. Er . . . long story, don't ask, but I kind of meddled in a *slightly* high-profile relationship and I think she wants to give me a taste of my own medicine. And anyway, it would be good for you, you know? Meet some of the people around town, show your face, talk up the B&B a little. And the band that's playing is indie folk, which has some overlap with country music—"

"I don't actually like country music," Derrick blurted.

"What?"

Derrick winced. "I don't actually like country music. I just play it to annoy you."

"You piece of shit!" Before Derrick could even react to the curse, tiny, feisty Ginsberg had somehow gotten him into a headlock. His face was mashed against Ginsberg's rib cage, and Ginsberg's tattooed knuckles were grinding into the top of his head. "Oh, you're definitely going out with me tonight. You fucking owe me, man! What the hell! Who the hell tortures a guy with country music just to watch them squirm? What is this, Guantanamo Bay?"

Derrick found himself laughing too hard—at Ginsberg's word vomit, at Ginsberg's fury, at the fact that Ginsberg had managed to headlock a man with a good foot in height, an extra working arm, and at least fifty pounds on him—to attempt fighting back.

And gathered as he was against Ginsberg's vibrant body, even in a headlock instead of an embrace?

Derrick wasn't sure he wanted to.

CHAPTER EIGHT

Ginsberg may have called it a not-date when he'd made his invitation, but he still dressed in his hipster finest. Jeans rolled up at the cuffs. Suede boots. Sweater vest. Plaid collared shirt—doing up buttons with one hand in a cast was a bitch, but he still managed it. Leather jacket, of course.

And despite it being a not-date, he still took extra care to adjust his packer in the mirror, making sure it looked just so. Full, but not obscene. Noticeable, but not the *first* thing you noticed.

Because he'd seen the way Derrick had looked at him this morning in the office. The way he'd *stared*. Not gawking at him like a scientific specimen or an animal in a zoo, but drinking him in, wanting him, recognizing him on that base, visceral level as a *man*.

Ginsberg discovered that he was more than happy to meet—and exceed—expectations on that front. Not that he needed to prove himself, not to Derrick or anybody, but that didn't mean he wasn't eager to show off. Especially if it got him laid. And he was definitely starting to get those vibes from Derrick now.

Or at least, he thought he was?

The guy was hard to get a read on. Sometimes he was charming and friendly and acted like he loved having Ginsberg around, and other times he was a cantankerous grump who played country music just to get on Ginsberg's nerves. And he really was a terrible host. If Ginsberg didn't know better, he'd think the guy was fucking up on purpose. But no, he was just that adorably incompetent.

Okay, sometimes adorable, sometimes infuriating. The burnt breakfast mostly leaned toward adorable, while the country music thing was infuriating. The inability to make a bed with any sort of precision was adorable. The still-unfixed touchy shower that by turns scalded and froze him, infuriating.

Where would tonight fall? When he came downstairs, which Derrick would be waiting?

No use worrying. He'd take the Derrick he was dealt, and he'd make it work. Kill 'em with kindness. The philosophy, while flawed, hadn't failed him on the Derrick front yet.

So he straightened his jacket, tried on his best unflappable smile in the mirror, and headed downstairs. The thing at the Stomping Grounds started at seven thirty, so he and Derrick had agreed to leave the house at quarter past. It was only seven now, but Ginsberg was too antsy to wait around in his room any longer. If he were the type of person to be concerned about seeming too eager, he'd have probably stuck it out and sauntered downstairs a few minutes after the time they'd set, but he wasn't.

Neither was Derrick, apparently, because when Ginsberg got to the top of the stairs, Derrick was already waiting at the base of them.

It was like the prom he'd never gone to—if proms were like the movies, anyway—except instead of feeling awkward and wrong in a huge glittery dress, Ginsberg was confident and feeling hot as hell.

Derrick gaped at him just like in the movies, though.

"I'm not late, am I?" Ginsberg joked. "Or are you that keen to go out with me?"

Maybe it wasn't the wisest decision to prod at someone as skittish as Derrick, but at least the forward approach gave him immediate insight into which Derrick he was dealing with tonight.

Prickly Derrick, judging by his disgusted scoff.

On the other hand, was that a blush Ginsberg saw on his cheeks and ears?

"Let's get this over with," Derrick growled, stomping toward the door. He swung a finger toward the living room, where Victoria Beckham sat perched on the back of the couch. "You. Watch the place."

Oh yeah, he was *definitely* blushing.

Dollars to donuts, his begrudging act was nothing but a cover for first not-date jitters. Well Ginsberg could *definitely* work with that.

The Stomping Grounds was just the kind of place Derrick imagined a person like Ginsberg would frequent. It was decorated with hideous modern "art," and the music on the store stereo was a band and genre Derrick couldn't identify—when you could actually hear it over the hiss of the espresso machine, that was.

The place was full of a typical Seattle crowd, all midtwenties kids in carefully selected ugly clothes and thick-rimmed glasses, each of them preening and posing and trying to out-hipster the other. There was even a poster on one wall advertising a Spoken Word Poetry Open Mic. At least Ginsberg hadn't invited Derrick to that. If he had, even his crushing guilt and helpless attraction wouldn't have been enough for him to say yes.

Ginsberg moved through this crowd easily, fitting in with the general vibe of the place and even greeting a couple of people by name.

He clearly belonged. The same couldn't be said of Derrick, who felt like a fucking asshole trying to mingle with a bunch of kids a decade and a half younger than him and into a style and a scene that was completely beyond his comprehension. He wondered what they'd think if they knew his buffalo plaid shirt was actual work wear.

Who was he kidding? Plaid shirt or no, they'd likely already pegged him for an outsider. He could sense their rejection.

What the hell was he doing here? He needed some fucking air.

But then a hand closed around his own, giving him a gentle, reassuring tug.

He looked up, and Ginsberg flashed him a brilliant, uncomplicated smile.

Well, that was one thing he *didn't* have in common with these other kids: as odd as he was, he was genuine. There was no posing, no fake aloofness, no sneer. Just his smile and kind eyes, inviting Derrick in.

"I just spotted a couple of the guys from *Wolf's Landing*," he said, not letting go of Derrick's hand. His palm was hot and rough, fitting perfectly in Derrick's own. "Want to meet them?"

"Not really," Derrick replied, determined not to give in to any of this madness, but he still let Ginsberg lead him through the chattering crowd.

"C'mon. They'll be glad to talk to someone who isn't a fan of the show. Give them a break from the hype."

"You think that's a thing Hollywood types even want?" Derrick asked.

"Oh come off it," Ginsberg scolded. "I thought you were above the whole 'grr, outsider bad' thing."

Defeated, Derrick grumbled, "I'm not sucking up to them. S'all I'm saying."

"Carter! Levi! Hey!" Ginsberg called.

Two men, sitting at a table on their own (with a third, much larger man at the table behind them, radiating *don't fuck with me or them*—the bodyguard, no doubt), glanced up and raised their hands in greeting. Derrick didn't recognize the younger of the two, but the older he recognized from . . . something. A movie, maybe. An action flick?

They were both unnaturally attractive, in that way actors were when you saw them up close. It was a little unsettling, but Ginsberg still had a death grip on his hand, so he wasn't going anywhere.

"Derrick, this is Carter Samuels, the star of *Wolf's Landing*. I'm his stunt double. And this is Levi Pritchard." He looked back and forth between them, as proud and eager as a puppy to be making introductions. "And this is . . . actually, I dunno. He's new."

"Alfonse," Carter said, flashing an apologetic smile at the guy—hmm, that was no doubt a story—who smiled back tiredly, completely erasing his sense of menace. "Two days after you left, a fan jumped a barricade on a location shoot and kind of, um, tackled me."

Carter blushed and Levi fumed as Ginsberg rushed out, "Ohmygodareyouokay?"

Carter nodded. "Didn't hurt me. Just really wanted a kiss I guess? Anyway, the suits came down hard on the bodyguard issue after that, at least when we're out and about." He leaned in and mock whispered, "Levi's *pissed*."

"Yes, Levi's pissed," Levi grumbled. "Don't need a damn shadow."

All three men seemed suddenly very uncomfortable about the whole thing, and Derrick thought to rescue them by changing the subject to . . . whatever it was Hollywood types might like to talk about, but Ginsberg beat him to it. "I'm sure you'll all get along great."

He offered his hand to the bodyguard. "Nice to meet you, Alfonse. Everyone, this is Derrick Richards. He runs the B&B I'm staying at."

Derrick moved to shake both their hands, and belatedly realized he was still holding Ginsberg's. Ginsberg must have realized it too, because he let out a nervous laugh and loosened his grip.

Derrick shook each man's hand in turn, although he had a feeling that as embarrassed and awkward as he felt just now, his grip probably wasn't as strong or as confident as he preferred.

Ginsberg to the rescue, again, with an icebreaker: "Levi," he groaned, diverting attention from any hand-holding. "Please tell me that is not a bottle of Coke. Please tell me you didn't come to a great independent coffee shop and order a *Coke*."

Carter laughed, easy and unself-conscious. "It's Coke," he confirmed. "I tried to convince him to at least try a mocha—"

"Coffee with training wheels," Ginsberg explained for Derrick's benefit.

"—But nope, Coke."

Levi seemed about to make some kind of witty and/or scathing reply when a woman's voice called "Carter Samuels! Oh my God!" They all turned, and a young woman in neon orange tights and a dress printed with owls hustled over, brandishing a cell phone. Alfonse stood up, tense, but Levi sharply waved him back. Looked like they still had some boundaries to work out between them. "It *is* you! And Levi too! Are you guys on a date? Can I get a picture? My Tumblr followers are gonna flip."

"We'll leave you guys to it," Ginsberg said, steering Derrick away before things got any more Hollywood-awkward.

Thank God.

"*Are* they on a date?" Derrick asked as they moved through the crowd and up to the counter.

"Uh, yeah." Ginsberg gave Derrick a slightly evasive look. "Didn't I— Yeah. Those coworkers I mentioned? The ones whose relationship I meddled in?"

"Carter Samuels and Levi Pritchard. The stars of *Wolf's Landing*," the woman behind the counter interrupted with a smirk. "Must be a special occasion for a recluse like Levi to be out in public, especially at an event like this. Either that, or Carter has him w-h-i-p-p-e-d. Hello, Ginsberg. Glad you could make it."

"Thanks," Ginsberg said, her snide expression seemingly washing off of him like water off a duck's back. "So. Tori. This here is Derrick Richards. He runs The Bayview B&B."

Tori startled. Stared. Finally, recognition dawned over her face. "Oh! *Ohhh*. Well, hell-o to you, Derrick."

What the hell was that supposed to mean? "Uh, hi," Derrick said.

Ginsberg put an elbow on the counter. "Can we get a—"

"Black coffee and an almond milk dirty chai." She smiled, then gave Derrick an inexplicably knowing grin. "You two go find a seat. Show's about to start. I'll bring the drinks out."

"What was that about?" Derrick asked after Ginsberg had paid their bill and they'd found an unoccupied table. Or rather, found a distressed old barrel that was apparently serving as a table in *this* place, anyway.

"She thinks I get *starry-eyed* when I talk about you," Ginsberg replied. He rolled said eyes.

"Do you?" Derrick asked.

Ginsberg, rather than getting flustered, stared straight back at him. "Do you want me to?"

Derrick flushed. He hoped that in the low light it didn't show.

Change of subject, change of subject... "Those two sure are popular with the locals," he said, gesturing in the direction of Carter and Levi's table, which was now surrounded by a small crowd of tittering groupies.

"Yep. Being in *Wolf's Landing* will do that for ya. And even if you weren't into their show, them being in a high-profile gay relationship definitely increased their standing in fandom."

Derrick wasn't going to touch that "high-profile gay relationship" point. He was still a little bit stuck in the mind-set that being gay drove most people *away*. But what did Derrick know? He was just some redneck queer, and really, the proof of Ginsberg's point was right there in front of his eyes. Carter and Levi's fans weren't just tolerant of their relationship, they seemed downright energized by it. "What about you?" Derrick asked.

"Believe it or not, I've never slept with or dated anyone I met with on set. Maybe because I have simpler tastes." He cast Derrick a meaningful look.

"Not that!" Derrick protested, shoulders rising. "I mean, you do that show too, but nobody's coming asking *you* for a photo."

"Why would they?" Ginsberg replied mildly.

"You do all the stunts! That's gotta count for something."

"Of course it does, but you don't get into my line of work for the fame or the attention. If I'm doing a stunt and people see *me*—as in, associate the stunt work with me and not Carter over there, then I've failed at my job. I'm still essential, but in a different way. You know?" He cleared his throat. "Doesn't mean I don't matter."

Having spent a decent chunk of his life up trees doing manual labor for no thanks and less pay, Derrick definitely understood. What he *didn't* understand was why Ginsberg was saying it like he was trying to comfort Derrick.

The front man of Smiths and Son Canning Co. was an anemic-looking midtwenties guy with an impeccably groomed handlebar mustache and porkpie hat. And a banjo. Ginsberg liked his style, but the minute he took to the stage, Derrick let out one of his signature disgusted noises.

"Just drink your coffee, old man," Ginsberg drawled before Derrick could start griping.

Good thing, too, because the crowd hushed. The rest of Smiths and Son Canning Co.—two more men and one woman—arrived on stage, did final sound checks, and launched without fanfare into their set.

Ginsberg had seen his fair share of bands perform live, and more than a few of them had played these exact same songs. Smiths and Son Canning Co.'s covers were pretty faithful, played well but without innovation or reinterpretation. As for their original songs, well, nothing life-changing, but nothing embarrassing, either. With the coffee and crowd, this rated as a pretty nice night out.

But there was more to tonight than just the music or the drinks or the atmosphere.

Derrick. Derrick was here.

And when Ginsberg caught Derrick drumming his hand and nodding his head and smiling slightly in the direction of the stage, Ginsberg's pretty nice night out turned into the best one he'd had in a very long time.

The twangs of the banjo and the singers' harmonics made everything seem so much more profound, like he and Derrick were starring in a low-budget indie movie. If so, this was definitely the scene leading up to the romantic climax.

When the band broke into a surprisingly spirited rendition of "40 Day Dream," the faux-bored audience came to life, stomping their feet and clapping out the beat. Ginsberg felt the thump before he saw it: Derrick, beside him, had joined in. Not quite as enthusiastically as the intoxicated twentysomethings twirling and jumping in front of the stage, but ever-reticent Derrick had his own scale when it came to outward shows of emotion, and joining in on an audience participation song must have put him right at the top of it. As good as the show on stage was getting, Ginsberg couldn't bear to drag his eyes off the guy.

The energized crowd swayed and sang along, building up to a frenzy. Derrick didn't stand, didn't dance, didn't cheer. He didn't need to; he expressed his enjoyment in his own way.

And if Derrick was drawn in by the infectious rhythm of the music, then Ginsberg was drawn in by Derrick.

The band played some good old-fashioned Johnny Cash to finish up their set, and now Derrick was pounding the table in appreciation. Grinning, eyes lit up, he turned to Ginsberg and whispered loudly, "Wish we could do something like this up at the B&B!"

A strange thing to say, considering the Stomping Grounds and the Bayview B&B were two very different types of business establishments, but Ginsberg got it: Music. Fun. Talk. *Life.* That was what Derrick wanted for himself and his business, and why shouldn't he? Must be lonely up there by himself. The place felt stale, and Derrick felt a little like a ghost and—

God, Ginsberg wanted to give him everything he wanted and everything he deserved. Help him have this feeling for his own every single day.

"Thanks for coming out, everybody," Tori said. She'd taken over the mic now that Smiths and Son Canning Co. were packing up. "And just to remind you all, we won't be having a performance next Friday because the shop will be closed all weekend for renos. But Friday after next, we'll be back and better than ever, so you better not miss it!"

No venue for the usual Friday performance?

Ginsberg grabbed Derrick's sleeve and gave it a tug, giving Derrick an *Are you thinking what I'm thinking* waggle of the eyebrows.

Derrick stared at him blankly for a second, then sputtered, "Absolutely not. Ginsberg, no. No. I mean it. No."

But behind his words, there was still that light in his eyes. His determined, scolding frown kept twitching at the corners.

Ginsberg just grinned right back.

And then he surprised himself as much as Derrick when he used that grip on the man's sleeve and all the eager optimism boiling up in him to pull Derrick in for a brief, meaningful peck on the lips.

Then, before Derrick could even begin to respond, Ginsberg took off through the dispersing crowd to find Tori. He had a gig to arrange.

CHAPTER NINE

Derrick was too stunned to even try to stop Ginsberg as he marched off like a one-man army through the crowd. The longer he sat there, though, the more he realized that maybe he didn't *want* to.

Why *should* he want to? Tonight had been great. The music, the crowd, the coffee, Ginsberg's company . . . Derrick refused to say he was lonely, but it sure was a relief to get out of that sad, dusty old house and into the real world. Hell, even without Ginsberg beside him, Derrick felt the energy of the crowd. To think he'd almost stayed home tonight. To think he'd almost driven Ginsberg from his life without even giving him—or this—a chance.

Levi and Carter waved cheerfully as they passed him on their way out, Alfonse hulking between the fans and one photographer trailing after them. "Nice to meet you!" Carter called over his shoulder with an extra wave.

If he sent Ginsberg away now, what else would he be giving up? He touched his lips, like he could still feel Ginsberg's there.

He liked Ginsberg. He did. There was no denying it anymore. No denying it ever, really. The kid may get on his nerves, but he liked that too. Liked the excitement of a little conflict, of bickering and butting heads with another guy. It was fun. Invigorating.

Fair play, but why did he have to fight Ginsberg *so* hard? And with such high stakes? Fighting over country music, that was fun. Trying to shut down his optimism . . . that was depressing.

So Ginsberg had thrown a wrench in his plans. Why couldn't he give the guy a chance to prove himself? Why did he have to stick to his guns about giving up on the B&B, even after a good reason not to had dropped into his lap?

Ginsberg believed in him. Thought they could turn the B&B around. Even had ideas on how to make it happen.

And here was Derrick, resisting at every turn, and why? Because he was afraid of failing? Because he was afraid of *succeeding*?

Why?

He jiggled his leg and shook his empty cup, watching the crowd thin. Waiting for Ginsberg to return. Missing him. And not just because he felt awkward sitting here alone. Missing him for his own sake.

And excited about what he *wasn't* going to miss out on now.

Ginsberg, when he finally swaggered back, didn't disappoint.

"Alright!" he announced, clapping his hands and rubbing them together.

Derrick tried very, very hard not to look too eager to hear what he had to say.

"I talked to Tori, and we're on for next Friday. She'll provide the coffee, we have to provide the venue and the food."

"Food?" Derrick said with a gulp.

"Food," Ginsberg repeated. "And venue. Which means we have a *lot* of work to do."

Work? Forget work, Derrick was gonna need a damn miracle.

And wouldja look at that, you got one of those standing right in front of you.

"I hope you know what the hell you're getting into," Derrick grumbled, but there was no helping the smile tugging at the corners of his lips.

A smile that Ginsberg must have seen, because he smiled back. Not one of his usual carefree grins, but something slower and softer, his eyelids low and his cheek tilted ever-so-slightly down to his shoulder.

Derrick's face flushed. "We should be heading home," he said. "Before my dog destroys anything."

Ginsberg blinked. Nodded. "Right. Yeah. Get an early start tomorrow."

Derrick nodded too, suddenly unable to make eye contact. "Uh-huh."

They walked in silence, avoiding one another's gazes, all the way out to Derrick's truck, which was parked down the block. They also spent the drive in silence. That brief kiss hung between them, making the space between Derrick's bucket seats feel even wider than usual.

What was the use of having a chatterbox like Ginsberg around if he wasn't even going to break the ice?

Derrick cleared his throat.

"That was fun," Ginsberg said.

"It was," Derrick replied.

More silence. Derrick drummed his hands on the steering wheel. Would have turned on the radio, normally, but considering he and Ginsberg's music-related interactions, it seemed like putting on some music would just make things *more* awkward. So driving in silence it was.

By the time they made it back to the B&B, he felt ready to crawl out of his own skin. Ginsberg didn't look much better. His movements as he made his way to the house were furtive and shy.

The tight front hall only made things worse. They kept bumping into each other, then making awkward slanted eye contact as they muttered apologies.

Ginsberg, small and lean as he was, finally slipped free. "Thanks for humoring me," he said with a lick of his lips, retreating backward up the stairs.

He turned, and Derrick watched him go, his chest squeezing horribly. "You too, kid," he called out at the last second. Ginsberg looked over his shoulder, and something about the sweet, unguarded nature of his expression tugged at Derrick. "I mean that. Thank you. For everything."

Ginsberg smiled.

He'd kissed Derrick.

Why the fuck had he kissed Derrick?

Staring up at the dim ceiling of his bedroom, Ginsberg absently swept a hand across his chest and down into his briefs. Just a cursory touch, but the fact that he'd done it at all was evidence enough.

Okay, he'd kissed Derrick because he was hot for him. Easy answer.

So then . . . why had he kissed Derrick without fully considering the consequences? He was lucky he wasn't out on his ass right now. Sure he was pretty much positive Derrick was at least physically attracted to him, but Derrick was also a skittish, withdrawn mess.

Ginsberg had to tread carefully. Read the situation. All good things in time. Bringing the guy out in public, introducing him to celebrities, arranging an event at his B&B, *and* kissing him all in one night? Ginsberg was lucky the guy hadn't fully retreated into his shell.

But then, maybe he had. It wasn't like their drive home had been anything other than massively awkward.

He grunted, pulling his hand from his underwear and rolling onto his side, where he curled up fetal-style on the edge of panic.

Yet Derrick had thanked him. Right at the end. And that had been genuine.

Maybe there was still hope.

But reminding himself of that didn't keep him from tossing and turning most of the night.

Didn't keep him from waking up an anxious mess, either.

Six a.m. and he leapt out of bed, driven by the illogical but compelling belief that if he didn't want to let Derrick spook and retreat back into himself, he had to act *fast.*

There really was a lot of work to do around the B&B, though, and an early start made perfect sense.

But it would be a flat-out lie to try to suggest *that* was the reason Ginsberg skipped his morning workout, took a lightning-fast shower, and threw on his clothes in record time. Because if it was, he'd have just gotten to work once he realized Derrick wasn't up and about yet. Which he didn't. Instead, in his urgency to get to Derrick before the doubt did, he headed down the hall to Derrick's room for the first time since coming here . . . and knocked.

A muffled, sleepy mutter was his reply.

What had happened to, *I don't sleep in, and I don't cater to people who sleep in, either*? Ginsberg knocked harder. "C'mon, big guy! Lots of work to do! Up 'n at 'em!"

No response. Not unless you counted the sound of someone tossing in bed as a response. But he wasn't giving up, not when it felt like his world hung in the balance. He rapped his knuckles. Thudded his fist. Alternated both to create little door knock drum solos. He was really getting into the rhythm of things when at last the mattress creaked and heavy footfalls shuffled toward him.

He puffed up his chest. Plastered his most obnoxiously cheerful smile on his face.

Should he have brought the guy a fresh mug of coffee? Would that look too desperate?

He gulped, smile wavering, as the door opened.

And very immediately, very *thoroughly*, understood Derrick's stunned, sputtering response to finding Ginsberg wearing nothing but a towel and a smile in the hallway on his first day here.

Wow.

Derrick was standing at the door in gray boxer-briefs, bleary-eyed and scratching his hip. He was . . . *wow*. A little bit of a paunch on him, but big powerful pecs, a handful each. Corded arms. Chest hair: a dark, dense thatch that thinned down to a line as it reached his navel, then thickened again at the waistband of his well-filled underwear. It made Ginsberg's mouth water.

Sexiest part was, Derrick wasn't even *trying*. When their positions had been reversed and Ginsberg had found himself in the hall before Derrick, he'd straightened up knowing full well what he was doing. What he looked like. How Derrick would react. He'd posed.

Derrick was still half-asleep. Probably didn't even know he was in a state of undress, or if he did, didn't realize who he was half-naked in front *of*.

Ginsberg flushed. "So um," he blurted out.

"Whaddya want?" Derrick rumbled.

To have that dick up my ass, Ginsberg's mind supplied. *Don't say that aloud. Don't say that aloud. Don't say that aloud.*

Never mind not voicing some serious dirty talk, he was struggling not to stare directly at the dick in question. The back of his neck was as hot as if the LA afternoon sun was beating down on it. "I, uh, you know, well, the . . ."

Derrick must have been waking up, because one eyebrow quirked and a lazy smile propped up one corner of his mouth. "Yes?"

"It's Saturday," Ginsberg finally managed to say.

"That's why I was planning on sleeping in." But Derrick didn't look angry so much as he did amused—at Ginsberg's expense.

If Ginsberg didn't nip this in the bud, *now*, there was no way in hell Derrick wasn't going to try to turn this encounter into full-on torture. He straightened his shoulders. Lifted his chin. Tried to summon up the will to be forceful and confident instead of a blubbering, turned on mess. "Well, change of plans. It's Saturday, and that means we officially have less than a week to get this place into tip-top shape for the Stomping Grounds thing."

"The wha—" A look of confusion, then recognition, then pure terror crossed Derrick's features. He fell against the wall of his bedroom. "Oh. Fuck. That."

"Yes, *that*," Ginsberg echoed smugly, basking in the shifting balance of power between them.

"I forgot . . . last night. Thought I'd—" A ruddy, patchy flush crept out from the sides of Derrick's neck. Ginsberg could see the exact moment he remembered their kiss. The way his mouth opened a bit, his tongue flicking out to tease his lower lip. The way his eyes widened ever so slightly, pupils flaring minutely. The way his belly turned concave and his chest expanded in a deep, bracing gasp.

Ginsberg smirked, stepping into the room, past the threshold. "Thought you'd what?" he teased. "Dreamt it?"

Derrick's brow furrowed. A deep growl rose from the bottom of his barrel chest. No time for Ginsberg to process what was happening, let alone react. Derrick *lunged*. Slammed Ginsberg to the bedroom wall, framed by his powerful arms and massive body. Leaned in, and Ginsberg was helpless to do anything but flatten himself against the wall and lift his chin, waiting to receive what Derrick had to give. Derrick's hot breath gusted across his face, and he squeezed his eyes shut, heart jackhammering.

But Derrick didn't kiss him.

CHAPTER TEN

W*ish I* was *dreaming, because if I was, I could damn well—*

But he wasn't, and he couldn't. He might have agreed to the damn concert, but Ginsberg would still be gone in a few weeks, would still be leaving Derrick alone with a failing business. Okay, maybe a marginally less-failing business. But alone. Alone was the point. He cleared his throat, forced himself to give Ginsberg a little space. "Less than a week, huh?" he said, and thanked his lucky stars his voice sounded suitably disaffected. He dusted his hands, backing off his prey abruptly. Breaking the strange spell between them.

Ginsberg, eyes still shut, knobby knees visibly wobbling, slumped against the wall. In relief or disappointment, Derrick couldn't tell.

"So I guess we better get to work cleaning the place. You—" he prodded Ginsberg's chest "—take the kitchen while I put some clothes on." *And get my shit under control.* Derrick may have had more outward composure than poor Ginsberg—who was now shuffling tight-cheeked out of the bedroom and down the hall like he actually had a tail to tuck between his legs—but inwardly, he was a goddamn wreck. Hungry, raw, wanting, angry at himself, turned on, invigorated, terrified. Each feeling as intense as the last.

Alive.

Suddenly it seemed like he had been sleepwalking through the last couple of lonely years, or like he'd been muffled by a fog, a haze he hadn't really comprehended until suddenly it was lifting. He was awake. He was seeing the world in color, in 3D, in high fucking definition and surround sound—all of it. The numbness was gone and it was overwhelming and exhausting and he should be more scared but he just *wasn't.* Not with Ginsberg here.

Fuck. He was completely losing his sense of perspective. Just because he may have decided to drop the whole drive-the-kid-out plan and the give-up-on-the-B&B plan didn't mean he had to trade them in for the fall-head-over-heels-with-flaky-out-of-towner plan. He sucked in a deep breath, blew it back out, but he couldn't dislodge the tangled mess of feelings that seemed to overstuff his chest cavity. Couldn't stop himself from picturing Ginsberg backed up against the wall looking needy as all hell with his chest heaving and his eyes squinched closed. Couldn't stop himself from picturing them together in the kitchen, cooking. From imagining music playing in the common room, and people. *People.* Even snide Seattle hipster types were a hoot once you gave them a chance. Would they come to the B&B, order food and drinks, chat and laugh and fall in love?

Like I'm falling in love?

Hell no. Derrick wasn't falling in love. Falling in love with an idea, maybe, a fantasy. Sure, Ginsberg the person was surprisingly nice to be around, but to Derrick he represented so much more. Optimism. Companionship. Success. The end of loneliness. Life, going on. That was what Derrick was in love with.

Still, Ginsberg the *person*, he liked. That was enough.

Derrick was going to seize this opportunity, take advantage of it for exactly what it was. And then when Ginsberg inevitably left—got his real job back, got his life back, got to move back into lodgings that weren't rock bottom priced—there'd be no regrets or heartbreak for either of them. Ginsberg would have gotten the satisfaction of meddling, Derrick would have gotten a reinvigorated business and a new chance to fulfill his parents' dream. Both better for their times in one another's lives, but still going their separate ways. A clean break.

Which Derrick wasn't going to be able to make if he slept with the guy.

Just look at the whole situation with Jim.

What a mess.

Forewarned was forearmed, though, and as long as Derrick kept his eyes on the prize, remembered the importance of boundaries, he'd be fine.

Definitely no more shoving the kid into walls.

But shit, could you blame him? The kid had been in his bedroom. Caught him off guard in that fuzzy place between dreams and wakefulness, where his judgment wasn't exactly up to par. And he'd wanted Derrick—had that wanting written all over his face and body. Hard not to respond. Impossible, even, especially considering the circumstances.

The kitchen, at least, would be neutral ground. And they'd be so busy cleaning that they'd have no time to get horny for each other.

He was gonna *need* to work him that hard if he hoped to get this place in shape for next Friday night.

Making a mental to-do list, he brushed his teeth, dressed in work clothes, and headed down the hall to the kitchen, where he could already hear Ginsberg banging around.

He wasn't cleaning, though. He was cooking.

Something that smelled out-of-this-world delicious. Victoria must have thought so too, because she stayed close by his feet as he moved about the kitchen.

Derrick fought the urge to sidle up behind him, press his groin to that round ass, wrap his arms around Ginsberg's waist and rest his head on Ginsberg's shoulder as he peered over it into the frying pan.

Such a domestic thing. Not one they could have, though. Not if Derrick wanted to keep things clean between them.

"What you doing?" he asked instead, lurking in the doorway and keeping his distance.

Ginsberg turned with a smile.

He was wearing Derrick's mother's old apron. Untied at the back, but still so . . . so . . .

It had frills. A rosy floral pattern. The bib portion of it was *heart shaped*.

Derrick didn't know whether to get angry, or to laugh. So he stood there, silently turning red.

"Not a good look?" Ginsberg asked with a cock of his head, expression coy and flirty despite the waves of . . . *whatever* radiating off of Derrick.

Before he could stop himself, before he'd even realized what he was going to say or why, he blurted out, "Don't you think it's a little bit girly, considering?" He gestured vaguely to Ginsberg's body.

Ginsberg's eyes narrowed to slits, all traces of humor gone. "If you think this apron's too girly for a man like me," he snapped, "you should see my vagina."

Derrick flinched. "Sorry, I—"

"Forget it," Ginsberg replied, turning back to the stove sharply. "I'm starting to figure you out. The whole can't-cook-can't-clean thing, is that all learned helplessness, then? An act? Can't let yourself be good at it because it's for *girls*?"

That was certainly the lesson he'd been taught at school, wasn't it? Was that why he resented this place and this job so much? Not because it had been foisted on him, or because his chosen career hadn't worked out?

Had he even picked forestry in the first place, or had he just gone for it because it was the obvious choice for a guy so hung up about acting like a guy? If so, then what really separated it from working here at the B&B, if not the gender line?

He couldn't speak. Didn't have an answer, anyway.

"Because if it is, you tell me right now. You *tell* me." Derrick had never seen somebody flip a pancake in anger before this moment. "And I won't waste any more time here, or on *you*." He practically spat it. "I can deal with your whole anxious masculinity thing when it's just *your* thing, your problem, your defect, whatever—never let it be said I don't love a charity case—but if you're gonna try and make it my problem, too, then that's not on. I'm not here to coddle your insecurities. I'm not here to try to impress your outdated understanding of masculinity. I'm not here to play *any* kind of part, in fact: I'm not here to live up to your 'standards' and I'm not here to be your failing example of manliness that you can measure yourself up against and always win, either."

There was a black hole in the pit of Derrick's stomach, and second by second, he was collapsing into it. His heart had already stopped beating.

Ginsberg rounded on him, brandishing his spatula. "I'm not here for you to look down on and depend on at the same time. So if that's what you want from me, or if you think you're gonna make a habit of undermining my gender, you tell me right now so I don't waste another second of love on you."

Love. He'd said— *Love. Jesus.*

But there was no reason to get worked up about any of it, because it wasn't romantic love, not the way Derrick had been thinking. Ginsberg was just referring to the love he gave the whole world, that giving nature, that way he carried light with him from place to place, making people happy, giving them what they needed. Love. He was a good fucking person, and he had a lot of it to give, and Derrick *needed* it. Him.

And now Ginsberg was standing here, fierce but hurting, ready to give up everything between them and everything they had, and Derrick realized he didn't find that petty or vindictive, he found it *brave.*

Derrick needed to be brave too, if he wanted to be worthy of any kind of forgiveness, and twice that to be worthy of Ginsberg's continued presence here. "I'm so sorry," he started, because that was the most important thing to say.

"You better be," Ginsberg sniffed, but it was obvious his anger was already escaping him. Was it difficult for him, being that damn easygoing? Did he frustrate himself? Put a lot of effort into his anger? Have to talk himself into not letting people walk all over him?

"I don't want you to leave," Derrick added. That was the second most important thing. "And I don't want you to play any parts for me, except for the part of 'inexplicably interested guy helping me get my shit together.'"

"*And* . . ." Ginsberg prompted, the hint of a smile on his lips.

"And I really do need to get my shit together. I don't know about learned helplessness, but I know I've got a damn bad attitude about this place and if I don't get that in check, all the help in the world won't save me."

"Right," Ginsberg said. He gave a nod. Didn't seem quite satisfied yet.

Derrick huffed. "My father—"

"Stop right there. You already let your father die without knowing who you really are. Are you going to let your fear of his disapproval dictate the rest of your life, too?"

Derrick recoiled. Had his relationship with his father been worse than he remembered? Or was Ginsberg just thinking of his own no-doubt shitty situation? "Actually, I was *gonna* say that when it came to manhood, my father's was never in doubt . . . and he still knew his way around the kitchen. And cleaning. And everything."

"Hmm," Ginsberg said, and his expression softened, becoming gentle and wistful. Derrick had the feeling that if he tried it, Ginsberg wouldn't reject an embrace.

"So I guess what I'm saying is . . . how about I get these dishes while you finish breakfast, and then after we eat we make up a plan of attack?"

Ginsberg swung his spatula menacingly. "Get to it then, dish bitch!" He grinned.

Derrick, suitably contrite, got straight to work washing up the dishes while Ginsberg put on some bacon for them. He hated raising his voice with the guy, calling him out like that, and not just because standing up to him jeopardized the roof over his head. The problem was, for all that Derrick was a shit, he wasn't spiteful or purposely cruel (okay, except for the country music), and no amount of people telling him "intent doesn't matter" could undo the fact that intent *did* matter to Ginsberg. Because sure, intent might not change the outcome, and he could still get hurt, but to him at least, ignorance and internalized fears hurt far, far less than malice or cruelty.

Regardless, he was proud of himself. A few years back, he'd have probably let microaggressions like that slide, even if they made him miserable, but not now. Good for him.

Didn't mean he didn't feel a bit guilty for Derrick's hangdog expression, though.

At least it was nothing a nice hot stack of pancakes couldn't fix, which simultaneously satisfied Ginsberg's base urge to make it all better *and* his more high-minded determination to not let himself be walked all over.

Which was important, because after this morning he and Derrick seriously needed to define their boundaries. Will-they-won't-they sexual tension may be great for sitcoms and police dramas, but less so for men living in close quarters.

Not that *he* was gonna be the one to open up that big can of worms. Not after risking his place here once today already.

For a good reason, for a damn good reason, he reminded himself.

Defining whether or not he and Derrick were going to get on with it and fuck really didn't rate on the same scale, so he'd save it for another time.

They weren't speaking to each other just now, anyway. Derrick looked mildly humiliated as he scrubbed dishes, and despite putting on a brave face, Ginsberg still felt too tender and shaky as he dirtied them to try making small talk. Every inch of him screamed to tell Derrick it was okay, that he was okay, and forgiven, or even joke around to break the ice, but Derrick's shameful silence was catching.

So Derrick silently, awkwardly washed dishes, and Ginsberg silently, awkwardly piled two plates full of food.

He thought they'd sit down to a silent, awkward meal, but then Derrick did the unthinkable: he met Ginsberg's eyes and flashed him a bashful smile.

"Thanks," he said.

"No problem," Ginsberg replied, relieved. "I'm pretty good at pancakes."

"I didn't mean the pancakes. Although those look amazing. I mean, thanks for taking me to task back there. It's been a long time since someone did that."

"I kind of had a feeling you needed some tough love." Ginsberg smiled at him, and Derrick smiled back, and just like that he felt a little less terrible about speaking up for himself. Derrick didn't hate him or think he was an oversensitive queen. He wasn't going to lose the roof over his head. Everything was okay.

"Haven't had much of that since my parents died. Haven't had much of anything, really. You know, after they . . . went, well, not that I ever had friends in the first place, but the people I *did* know on some level, I didn't exactly put out much of an effort to keep them around, I guess. People around town, they gave me a lot of leeway because I was grieving, but the more careful they had to be around me, the more they kept their distance, and then suddenly I was alone. And the people who didn't leave me behind, I just . . . drove them off."

"You know, my parents aren't *dead*, but I get it. You have problems, and people support you. But then those problems don't disappear in a timely fashion, and they get tired of always being there. Even if they're not callous, they just drift away." He reached across the table, brushing his fingertips over the knuckles of Derrick's balled fist before drawing carefully back again. "When people are doing that, it's easy to convince yourself you don't deserve support, or that you're better off alone because then at least nobody's disappointing you and you're nobody's burden."

Derrick nodded, stoic and silent. He hadn't touched his pancakes.

"I didn't know you before your parents died, but I'm gonna hazard a guess that even before you were grieving, you didn't exactly surround yourself with people."

"That's an understatement," Derrick said with a bitter chuckle.

"I must seem like an alien to you, being as social as I am." Ginsberg calling himself social, now there was an understatement. "But you know what, even introverts need *somebody* some of the time. Even if it's just someone to break them out of their very sad lonely echo chamber and tell them to get their shit together."

"I did need that," Derrick admitted. "But since I'm putting myself out there already, I might as well say I think you're more to me than that."

"O-oh?" Ginsberg suddenly found it hard to breathe.

"Having you here in this house, it's like there's music playing all the time."

Ginsberg very pointedly didn't bring up Derrick's country music prank.

"Like you know, when you're home alone and you turn on the radio, not to listen to but just to have some noise so the place feels a little less *empty*? That's you. That's what you do. Even when you're not in the same room or talking to me or anything, I can feel you here. You change this place. My parents are still dead, but me and this house . . ." He stared Ginsberg directly in the eye and his expression made Ginsberg want to stiffen and straighten his posture and melt into a puddle on his chair all at the same time. "You make me feel like maybe *we* could come back to life."

There was that urge to kiss him again. Ginsberg forced himself not to act on it, not until he knew for sure where the line was drawn. "That's the plan, yeah. So eat up, we've got a job to do."

Both of us. Together.

For the next seven weeks before his cast came off, anyway.

CHAPTER ELEVEN

Ginsberg had grand plans, Derrick realized as they ate. Halfway through their meal, he trotted out of the room and came back with a notebook and pen. At the top of the page, he scrawled in chicken scratch, TO DO BY FRIDAY NIGHT, and underlined it three times.

Top of the priority list was to clean everything and everywhere. Get the kitchen up to a standard that wouldn't fail a health inspection, but more than that, dust and declutter and make the whole house look less like a dated relic fallen into disrepair.

Which was fair enough. Derrick hadn't been able to bring himself to change anything from the way his parents had left it. Unfortunately, in trying to preserve their presence, he'd let the whole place get stale, trapped in time. It had to be done, Derrick knew, but as determined as Ginsberg was to help him move forward and get back on his feet, he also wasn't ruthless. He touched Derrick's hand, light and brief. "We'll find ways to make it yours while still keeping your parents' memory alive. Okay?"

"Okay." It was hard keeping the emotion out of his voice. Derrick hadn't voiced that fear; it hadn't even really fully formed in his mind *to* voice, but Ginsberg had predicted it would be a concern anyway.

Because Ginsberg cared.

After the cleaning, they'd need to come up with some branding, find a way to make the event "work with the venue," as Ginsberg put it. Play to the B&B's strengths, then use that knowledge to advertise and get the word out and get the people coming *in*. It was kind of amazing how smart Ginsberg was about these things. Made sense, though, since he'd been surrounded by creatives for most of his life and career.

Of course they'd rubbed off on him. That was what happened when you didn't hide alone in your sad empty house.

"You don't have a stage or adequate seating or as big an acoustic space as the coffee shop, so we can't exactly bill it as a concert or a show on the flyers, but what if we call it a house party?" Ginsberg cast a look around the dining room. "The band's playing in here maybe, and there's drinks and coffee and food where you can be right in the center of the music, or you can take your drink and go to the living room for some quiet conversation or . . ." His eyes twinkled. "*Or* you can go upstairs and make out."

"As long as they pay an hourly rate for the room," Derrick grumbled.

He thought Ginsberg would call him stingy or greedy or try to call him down for wanting to run a brothel, but he just grinned instead. "Love it! I'll bring some ideas to Tori, see if she can get one of her indie kids to do up some cool posters and flyers we can distribute. We'll need something catchy to get a good turnout and attract the right crowd."

As scary and kind of crazy as his ideas were, they were also strangely invigorating. Like maybe he was just the change this place—and Derrick—needed. What good was a change if it wasn't a little frightening to contemplate, right? Derrick had tried keeping things the same and failed. Why not let Ginsberg shake things up, even if it meant a house full of hipsters?

Ginsberg cared. He wouldn't do anything that wasn't necessary. He wouldn't go too far for Derrick to follow. Derrick had to trust that.

"So it's all set," Ginsberg said, rapidly drumming his pen against his notebook. So much enthusiasm and energy. "Which brings us to . . ." They both winced at the same time. "Food," Ginsberg finished.

"I suppose ordering pizzas won't fly," Derrick asked.

"Not if we want to use this as an opportunity to increase the B&B's profile. We have to serve them something *fucking good*, Derrick. Something that has them raving about the hospitality here. Suggesting it to all their backpacker friends and their parents and their backpacker friends' parents."

"So we're fucked, then." He slumped back into his chair, crossing his arms.

Ginsberg slid down in his own chair and gave Derrick a nudge with his foot under the table. "Come on, man. Buck up. So you're a bad cook. It's a skill. You can learn it."

Derrick raised his eyebrows. "In a week?"

"Less than, technically, but okay. Let's assume it's gonna take longer than a week to teach you to do a good hot breakfast. Nobody's gonna want breakfast at a house party, anyway, so you've got time to figure that out. Can you cook anything else, maybe? Dinner food? Snacks? *Pastries*?"

"What, like chocolate croissants and danishes and stuff? That was all Jim's thing. Went straight to his ass, he used to say."

Ginsberg lunged forward across the table. "Who's Jim?" *Tap tap tap tap tap tap* went his pen.

Oops.

Derrick sighed his defeat. "He's my ex. Pretty sure I gained thirty pounds when he was living here. He did do some damn good baking."

"Oh really? So, as your ex, would you say he and you. . ."

"Are on speaking terms?"

Ginsberg nodded rapidly, so excited to hear Derrick's answer he didn't even try to play it as cool as would normally be expected when talking about such a sensitive topic.

Derrick strangely appreciated that, as awkward as it could have been.

Ginsberg couldn't fake disinterest out of caution, ergo he probably couldn't fake all this enthusiasm and caring and investment, either. He was what he was.

What he was . . .

"Yeah, we're on speaking terms. He dog-sits Victoria Beckham for me, actually."

"Oh!" Derrick could just see the lightbulb flick on.

"Yep."

"And he can bake?"

Derrick groaned, and fuck, he wanted to say no to this whole thing, he didn't want to open this particular Pandora's box, didn't want to invite Jim back into his life, didn't want Jim and Ginsberg to meet, but how could he say to Ginsberg now? "He can bake."

"And he could come over maybe? Teach us his ways?"

"I dunno about teaching *me* a damn thing, but he'll definitely come over."

"Why do you sound like you're dreading the possibility? I thought you said you guys were okay?"

"Oh, you'll see."

It wasn't that Ginsberg didn't trust Derrick not to chicken out . . . but Ginsberg really didn't trust Derrick not to chicken out. So he stood by and made *sure* that he called his ex about the possibility of a baking lesson.

Derrick was too much of a spoilsport to turn the phone on speaker, but judging by the high-pitched noise coming through the receiver and the way Derrick flinched away from it, Jim was downright ecstatic to help in their mission.

"Thursday. Uh-huh, the place should be clean by then. Thursday. Uh-huh. Uh-huh. Well, Friday night. Okay. Okay." He paced the small kitchen, phone tucked between his shoulder and his ear while he swept the floor and Ginsberg took an inventory of their cleaning supplies. "Uh-huh. Yeah. Okay. Okay. Bye. Okay. Bye. *Bye*!" He hung up with a massive scowl.

"Well?" Ginsberg asked, purposefully combating Derrick's dour expression with his own chipper tone.

"Well, it cost me my dignity, but he's in."

"Awesome!" Ginsberg punched the air. "Trust me, your dignity will be worth it when you get a slew of reviews online praising how good the food here is."

"Hmm," Derrick muttered noncommittally.

"So he's coming by Thursday?" Ginsberg prompted, trying to keep up his enthusiasm. "That works, we should be cleaned up by then."

"And Friday," Derrick said.

"And . . . ?"

"Yeah. He's coming to give us a lesson Thursday, but then he'll come by Friday to *supervise*. Says I'm a shit student and his reputation's on the line, so he wants to be there."

"Okay, that's fine," Ginsberg said, not sure how to respond to Derrick's eye roll. "I mean, that's good, always nice to have another pair of hands."

"So you say. Until you realize he's just desperate to spend time with me and he's also the worst third wheel in the history of third wheels."

Third wheel? Ginsberg sucked in a sharp breath, his heart stuttering like he was fifteen again. "Wh-what do you mean, third wheel? That would imply we're dating, you know?"

Derrick flushed. "Well we're not, but that won't stop him from proving the saying three's a crowd."

That flush, combined with the vehement *Well we're not*, had Ginsberg thinking along the lines of The Lady Doth Protest Too Much, so it was with a particular glee that he added, "Too many cooks in the kitchen, too," and finished Derrick off with a wink.

"Lord help me."

"You better ask Satan and Santa Claus, too." Ginsberg balled up the cleaning supply list and tossed it at his chest. "You're gonna need all the help you can get."

Derrick stooped, picked up the crumpled list, and carefully reopened it. "Satan, huh? I thought I was already in his unholy presence?"

"Keep it up, bud. See where it gets you."

He could have sworn Derrick flinched at the unspoken threat. He should have played it cool because he'd only been joking anyway, but some part of him was determined to speak up: "Teasing, Derrick. Just teasing. I won't leave you in the lurch." He laughed, gesturing to his bum arm. "After all, where the hell am I gonna go, huh?"

"Heh," Derrick replied, and despite Ginsberg's efforts didn't seem cheered up even a little.

CHAPTER TWELVE

Derrick had never cleaned so much in his *life*. Every time he thought he'd gotten an area or even an object up to snuff, Ginsberg would wander in and give him that pained expression that said, *I know you're working hard, but this isn't enough.*

He was trying to be nice, Derrick knew that, or as nice as he could be while still keeping his promise of helping the B&B be the best it could be, but somehow that little wince was a thousand times worse than a hundred sweaty power-tripping foremen telling him to get his fucking act together and do better.

Worse than the cleaning—the vacuuming and the dusting and the scrubbing and the organizing—was the "decluttering." It wasn't all bad: tossing the newspapers and flyers he had lying around everywhere was a relief more than anything, but then it came time to start thinning out his parents' possessions, and that was when it got rough.

Ginsberg was gentle with him, which once again only made it worse. "The good news," he said, "is that I think you can keep a lot more than you might otherwise. There's a certain kitschy appeal to this place that should have a certain crowd coming out in droves."

"So we can just dust it all and leave it as is?" Derrick asked, a little too hopefully, then coughed. "I mean, not that I'm attached to any of this crap or anything, but the less I gotta haul to the curb, the better."

Ginsberg raised an eyebrow. "I don't think so," he said. "Right now what you've got is great, but it's *too much*. The good stuff needs room to breathe, space to get noticed, you know? You just need to edit. Thin it out. Let what's left really shine."

What's left.

What a sad fucking phrase.

His whole parents' lives, and what was left?

Porcelain dolls and watercolor paintings. Dis- and reassembled antique radios. Stacks of home design magazines. Glass soda bottles. Faded fake flowers. Ledgers and bills and receipts and invoices, all dumped into bankers' boxes. Shoeboxes full of family photos, never framed or put in albums.

Their clothes.

Ginsberg found a few boxes and labeled them KEEP, DONATE, STORE, and TRASH. He set them out in the middle of the living room, then dusted his hands, saying, "I'm gonna work on some flyers. Leave you to it, okay?"

Part of Derrick was happy to not have an audience for what was to come. The other part—

"Can you stick around, maybe?"

Ginsberg, who'd already made it to the living room's doorway, paused. Cast Derrick a look over his shoulder. His expression seemed . . . pitying. Definitely pitying.

Derrick scoffed back at him. "I mean, you're the one who knows what these hipsters like. Otherwise I'm just gonna trash it all."

Ginsberg's frown at that was gone almost as soon as it had appeared. "Well I *am* the King of Kitsch. In this house, anyway." He sauntered back into the room, dropping onto the sofa with Derrick. "Let's start with the obvious," he said, gesturing to the stacks of magazines.

The magazines went into the TRASH box. The fake flowers were without question to be donated, but Ginsberg said to keep the various flea market vases they'd been sitting around in all these years. The porcelain dolls, which Derrick couldn't bear to part with at that moment—*"my mom always loved these creepy fuckin' things and I'm pretty sure if you dumped them now she'd haunt you"*—went into storage. As for the radios?

"Definitely keep. I think we should display them all. Does he have any more anywhere? In the shed? The attic? Workshop?"

"All of the above," Derrick said.

"So, *so* cool," Ginsberg praised, not a trace of irony or condescension in his tone.

They kept his mother's handmade quilts, but the towels and sheets all got donated or torn up into cleaning rags.

Room by room, they worked with a little less efficiency than was likely ideal, but Derrick was full of memories and Ginsberg was full of his usual nosiness, so it seemed like every second object to be sorted had to come with a story.

That hideous crocheted toilet roll cover doll that Derrick had once "drowned" in the toilet bowl. The little wooden set of Dutch souvenir clogs his father had bought at a local yard sale, having never set foot in Europe. The model airplane Derrick had insisted on one Christmas and then never bothered to assemble. His mother's wedding veil.

Ginsberg stuck by him the entire time, asking questions, listening attentively, supporting his decisions to keep or trash or donate.

Funny: Derrick had been holding on to all this stuff for so long, but he hadn't thought of the memories or emotions associated with any of it until now.

Now he was holding everything up to the light and telling Ginsberg what it all meant.

And somehow, reliving the history of the various trinkets let him give them up just as often as it reminded him of reasons to keep them.

It made a kind of sense, really. Once, Derrick only had the object to share each memory with. Now he had Ginsberg.

Ginsberg, who clasped his shoulder or nudged his knee or squeezed his hand as he spoke, making him feel a little less ashamed by the way he choked up periodically. Ginsberg, who never begrudged him the time or the effort. Ginsberg, who never abandoned him.

With Ginsberg's help, by Thursday he barely recognized the place. Or himself. It wasn't just the house that had gotten a thorough cleansing, as it turned out.

He liked the look of the antique radios—his father's private collection—brought from their various dusty hiding places and put on display all around the house in positions of pride. He liked the way his mother's inherited china gleamed in her now-decluttered cabinet. He liked how welcoming the beds looked with the cozy well-loved quilts but fresh sheets.

He liked his clean, organized kitchen that maybe even *he* could cook in.

They hadn't made it to the garage or the office or Derrick's bedroom—*yet*—but everywhere a guest could see was absolutely *immaculate.*

It was like a whole new B&B . . . except it wasn't, because so much of his parents' personality still remained. Their collections, their precious things, their wallpaper choices and their art, it was all still there. Just minus the dust.

And the crocheted toilet roll doll, who had made her trip to the local thrift shop now that Derrick knew her story was safe with Ginsberg.

The newly clean B&B was energizing. The flyers Ginsberg had designed and handed out were inspiring. The word about the buzz from Tori was reassuring. Derrick was almost looking forward to tomorrow night. Almost.

He had to get through today first.

And Jim.

Who he knew he should be thanking his lucky stars for, who he *knew* was going to be instrumental in Friday night's success.

But God he'd been enjoying his one-on-one time with Ginsberg. Telling those stories, even the slightly emotional ones—shit, they were totally emotional since they were about his dead parents and all—and having Ginsberg listen without judgment or dramatics, had felt damn good. As well as Jim knew him, he couldn't let his guard down in the same way.

Also, there was no way in hell they could keep up the borderline flirting with Jim around. If Derrick so much as looked at Ginsberg wrong, Jim would be all over them both, as yappy and hoppy as Victoria Beckham ever was. Cooing and pawing and making a damn scene.

Or hissing like a viper out of jealousy.

Hell, even if the guy miraculously didn't act like a fool one way or another, he'd still be elbowing in on the oasis Derrick and Ginsberg had so carefully built for themselves the past few days. Derrick knew he had to give that isolation up in order to have their "house party," and would continue having to give it up if the party succeeded in drawing new guests to the B&B, but that knowledge made these last days alone with Ginsberg all the more precious.

And just when did a loner like Derrick consider his time with perky busybody Ginsberg "precious"?

Damn, maybe some time with Jim wasn't such a bad idea. Remind him of why he'd chosen to live his life alone in the first place.

The way Derrick talked about the guy, Ginsberg expected Jim to be one of those insufferable shits that rubbed your face in how much you "owed" them, to the point that you resolved to never ask them for anything ever again, even if it turned out you needed a kidney to live and they were the only one in the world with a match.

What he *didn't* expect was to be greeted by a slim, squealing man with a massive reusable grocery box full of baking supplies in his arms. Who shoved that box of baking supplies against Derrick's chest and immediately enfolded Ginsberg in a tight, genuine hug. Then pressed a kiss to each of Ginsberg's cheeks.

"Thank you, thank you!" Jim trilled, keeping his hold on Ginsberg as he did. "Thank you so so so much for everything you're doing for Dick!"

"*Jim*," Derrick protested, pained, but Ginsberg waved him off. With guys like Derrick he respected personal boundaries, but when it came to huggers like Jim, he proudly gave as good as he got, so he squeezed Jim and kissed his cheeks right back.

"Thank *you*," he corrected when they finally pulled off of each other.

Derrick gave them both a suspicious look, still holding the overpacked box Jim had dumped on him.

Jim winked, then turned. "Now wheeere is my little princess?" he called. "Vickie? Vickie! Vickie!"

Victoria Beckham was well trained enough to come when called, but wasn't well trained enough not to immediately start hopping and barking and baring her teeth.

"There she is!" Jim cooed, not the slightest bit put off by her aggression. "There she is! Who's a good girl, huh? Who's my little princess fashionista?" He crouched, hands on his knees, and made loud kissing noises as Derrick sighed and lugged his burden to the kitchen. "Come here little princess, Uncle Jim has a cookie for you, you want a cookie? You want a treaty cookie?" He reached into his jacket pocket and produced one of those froufrou high-end dog biscuits with icing and rainbow sprinkles. Victoria Beckham, ears still pinned back, approached him warily but steadily. "Uncle Jim made it just for you, yes he did! Yes he did! Just for my little princess!" She snapped the treat right out of Jim's fingers. Ginsberg was surprised he even still *had* fingers, after that. But Jim just laughed, watching her scamper out of the hall and into the living room. "Bye-bye my spoiled little princess!" he called after her.

He beamed a big smile at Ginsberg.

"You make gourmet dog biscuits?" Ginsberg asked, offering him a hand up.

"It's a little side project, yeah. I mean, all my baking is. My day job's in accounting." He scrunched up his nose in disgust. "I work Monday to Friday, usually, but I took a personal day to help Derrick out."

"Thank you for doing that," Ginsberg said. "I mean it. We've been working really hard trying to get this place ready for the event tomorrow night, and you're a big part of what we're planning."

"Well I know Derrick didn't tell you to say that," Jim replied with a twinkle in his eye. He had little fine lines that deepened when he smiled, his age at odds with his bleached hair and low-slung skinny jeans. Ginsberg loved every inch of him. "But who cares what he thinks, huh? I can see who's in charge here now."

Ginsberg blinked, recoiling slightly. "It's not—"

"I'm just teasing you, boy. I've known Dick long enough to know he can't be forced or strong-armed or guilt-tripped or blackmailed or even boipussy whipped."

"Right," Ginsberg agreed, relieved.

"But I'd be lying if I wasn't saying you've obviously been a good influence on the guy. I mean, come on, look at this place, it looks great! And you got him to leave the house? And to actually try to get some customers in?"

"Hey, I can *hear* you," Derrick rumbled from the kitchen.

"Of course you can, sweetie. You think I talk this loud because I *don't* want to be heard by all and sundry?" He slipped a hand into Ginsberg's elbow. Which . . . Ginsberg hadn't remembered holding out for him. But now that they were linked, it felt just fine. "Come on, he's probably going crazy in there all impatient and left out. Last thing we need is for me to try to teach you two how to make gourmet donuts while Dicky is in a full class-five sulk."

"Can *still* hear you!"

"Gourmet donuts?" Ginsberg asked.

"All the rage right now. You do not want to be *that* party, serving cupcakes like it's still 2005 let me tell you."

"I was thinking more along the lines of, I dunno, cookies . . ."

"Cookies? Oh no, no, no. Honey, no. This is Dicky's big day. I am pulling out all the stops. I even brought a pound of bacon."

Derrick, who had started emptying Jim's big box onto the countertop, gave them a puzzled look. "Bacon? I thought we weren't doing breakfast?"

"Oh, *honey*." Jim eyed Derrick with the kind of lofty pity Ginsberg suspected he usually reserved for drag queens with unsteady eyeliner hands. "Watch and learn."

CHAPTER THIRTEEN

Apparently, the bacon was for the donuts. Jim didn't even let Derrick touch it, which was fair enough, since despite being the owner of a bed-and-*breakfast* he was absolutely fucking abysmal at cooking it properly.

Ginsberg, on the other hand, made it look easy, dredging the bacon in brown sugar and cinnamon and then putting it into the oven to crisp up. Jim whacked Derrick's hand with a spoon when he tried to snag a slice.

"No. Sit. Here." Jim shoved a mixing bowl into his arms, then piled a whisk and a set of measuring spoons and cups inside it.

What was he, a dog?

Except Jim never spoke so firmly to Victoria Beckham, not even when she was doing him grievous bodily harm.

"You can make the batter. Can't burn *that*. Just, for Mimi's sake follow the recipe, would you?"

Ginsberg laughed, all conspiratorial-like.

"You too, lovebird. Just perch on that chair next to Dicky and triple-check his measurements. I swear, it'll say one cup and he'll put in three purely out of spite."

"I do not—"

"Ah ah ah! Now watch, this is *very* important." He talked them through warming milk to prep the yeast—*SAF only, don't get the cheap stuff*—then ordered Derrick through melting butter and beating eggs. "Good and hard," Jim urged, then added, "Faster," winking at Ginsberg for some reason, who blushed to the tips of his ears.

When the eggs and butter were whisked together, Jim dumped them into the electric mixer. The milk and yeast—which had gotten all bubbly and weird and kind of gross—went in after. Jim waved for Derrick to turn it on, but, uh-uh, not a good idea.

"You want that shit painting the kitchen walls?"

Jim whapped him with a spoon again. "Don't be such a baby. Set it on low, and put the beaters in slowly. *Eeeeeease* it in, you know how to do that." He winked at Ginsberg again, and Derrick briefly entertained the idea of throttling him and burying him in the backyard. At least Ginsberg seemed to take Jim's behavior in stride. "Go on."

Remembering Ginsberg's whole "learned helplessness" speech, Derrick very precisely, very carefully—possibly with his tongue poking out of his mouth in concentration—followed Jim's instructions.

And lo and behold, the kitchen was not painted.

"See?" Jim practically squealed, clapping his hands. Ginsberg shouldered up next to Derrick, peered into the bowl of neatly creaming ingredients, and patted him on the back with his good hand.

"What's next?" Ginsberg asked while Derrick was too busy being amazed that every surface of the room wasn't covered in slimy yeast crud.

"Dry ingredients." Jim fished a recipe card—complete with smiling comic donut with floating eyebrows—from the box he'd brought in and handed it to Ginsberg. "Measure, mix together, then incorporate slowly into the stand mixer and beat with a dough hook for about ten minutes. Once it's mixed, we let it chill a few hours. And *while* it's chilling, it's on to the fun part: Toppings. Glazes. Starting with some candied crumbled bacon, yum!"

"Candied bacon," Derrick echoed in disbelief.

"Trust me, that stampede of hipsters you've got coming in tomorrow night are going to go gaga for it. And if they only liked bacon *before* it was cool, I've got a little pink peppercorn confection that should send even the most cynical and jaded of taste buds to the moon and back."

"*Pink*," Derrick echoed again. And *confection*? He'd never used the word *confection* in his life and could've died happy that way. *Pink confections* were his mom's domain. Jim's domain. What the fuck was he *doing*?

"Something wrong with pink?" Ginsberg asked, and even lost and confused as Derrick felt, there was no missing the edge to his voice.

"Oooooh," Jim drawled, eyebrows flying to the edge of where his hairline used to be. Reacting with all the exaggerated drama of a man who had no clue how serious a sore spot that little question represented.

"No," Derrick sputtered, "Just always thought peppercorns were black, was all."

Ginsberg sniffed, clearly not convinced.

Jim, oblivious, carried on business as usual with a theatrically put-upon sigh. "He thought peppercorns were black!" His eyes drifted heavenward. "Why in the name of Cher is *he* the one who gets to cook for a living while I'm stuck balancing books and getting elbow deep in tax loopholes? I'm a bottom, dammit!"

"Beats getting hit by cars for a living," Ginsberg said, pushing a bag of flour against Derrick's chest with entirely more force than was necessary. White powder puffed all over everything, and Derrick coughed but took the hint and sat down to measure it out.

"Sssssss," Jim hissed sympathetically, eyes on Ginsberg's cast.

Ginsberg's eyes were on Derrick's hands, though, and softer now as he watched Derrick very carefully measure the flour. "Nah, I was just teasing. I really do love it. To be honest, I'm thankful every day that I could still find work after . . . I mean, I'm kind of a little guy, you know? Not exactly stunt-double material for your average male action star."

Derrick winced as he leveled off his second cup of flour. Ginsberg *had* found work despite his size. Steady work, even, and not just for anyone—no, for the male lead on a hit TV show. And as soon as his arm healed, he'd be going back to it. Away from this train wreck of a B&B and Derrick's train wreck of a life. As if to prove his own point, he dumped the flour in the bowl too fast, coating the table and his hands in a poof of white dust, and Ginsberg frowned.

"Ohhh!" Jim cooed. "You're on *Wolf's Landing*? Derrick hadn't told me anything about you apart from the fact that you like dogs and you're staying long-term. He never tells me anything." He fixed Derrick with one of his fake glares, then plastered a smile on as he turned to Ginsberg again. "I am *such* a fan. I've been trying to convince Dicky for-*ever* that we should do a Monday night thing and watch it together. I even bought the first two seasons on DVD just to loan to him."

"Thanks for supporting the show," Ginsberg said with a soft, genuine smile. He had a measuring spoon pinched in the fingers of his casted hand, a container of salt in the other. His eyes darted between the spoon and Jim. "And yeah. I'm a stunt performer. Thus the whole hit-by-cars thing. I don't just jump in front of vehicles for, like, lawsuit money for a living or anything." He laughed, and so did Jim.

Derrick thought he was supposed to laugh too, but he couldn't manage it.

"Is it good money?" Jim asked. "I mean, it can't be *that* good if you're staying here."

"Hey!" Derrick snapped, but Jim just shrugged him off. Unfortunately, he couldn't spend much time being angry at Jim when suddenly all his anger was turning toward himself for never thinking to ask Ginsberg about any of this.

Ginsberg put down the salt container, leveled off the spoon with the back of a knife, and dumped it atop the flour. "Honestly? Hour by hour, it's so good I'm almost embarrassed about it. But then I have to remind myself that in this line of work, you spend way more time *looking* for work than actually *doing* work. So most of your hours you're not actually getting paid. I mean, I got *way* lucky with a regular gig—for season 4, my agent negotiated a season contract, rather than the usual day-by-day or week-by-week setup. But then—" He made a sound like an explosion and coupled it with jazz hands, then pointed to his cast. "So now I'm getting workers' comp instead of a regular paycheck. And residuals from the first two seasons are kind of shit because I *was* a day player then, and not on screen as often. And my agent takes fifteen percent of everything, of course. Plus I've got some pretty serious medical debts to pay off—not to mention every other kind of debt from when work was thin—so the money disappears fast."

"But you're staying afloat?" Jim asked, laying a tender hand on Ginsberg's shoulder. Derrick had forgotten that: Jim's gentle, unassuming compassion, so quiet and safe underneath his theatrics. Derrick had been on the receiving end of that same expression more times than he could count, from all the way back in school when the kids were particularly mean, to the months after his parents died. He never did give Jim enough credit for that side of him.

Ginsberg shook off the momentary melancholy like a dog coming in from the rain, and smiled brightly. "I am now, yeah. Thanks to Derrick here."

Jim nodded like a bobblehead. "Good. Good. Well, as much as I bitch, I'm pretty good with numbers and tax laws, so if you ever want some pro bono advice hit me up."

Ginsberg's grin at that was warm and genuine and made Derrick unreasonably jealous. Ginsberg wasn't his, after all. Would never *be* his. They weren't even fucking. And if Ginsberg knew what Derrick was thinking right now, he'd no doubt call Derrick a caveman or some shit like that for thinking in terms of *mine* and *not mine*. Which . . . was fair, he supposed. Ginsberg wasn't an object to be possessed or collected like Dad's antique radios, and shame on him for thinking that way, even for a moment. Ginsberg wasn't for display, and he fit in Derrick's life no better than Dad's antique radios.

Derrick scowled into the mixing bowl and stirred the salt into the flour. This was stupid. This was *beyond* stupid. Why had he ever agreed to let Ginsberg bring all his yuppie Hollywood friends to some yuppie Hollywood music performance anyway?

"You gonna stir that flour forever, Dicky, or are we gonna make donuts?"

Derrick offered him a guilty smile and stirred in the last dry ingredient—sugar—before taking the bowl over to the mixer. He went to dump it into the wet stuff when Jim grabbed his arm and shouted, "*Wait*! Not all at once—are you *insane*?"

Obviously.

"I got this," Ginsberg said to Jim, as tenderly as Jim had been with him before. He gently extracted Derrick's arm from Jim's hand, then put his own good hand on Derrick's wrist. The breath gusted right out of Derrick at Ginsberg's touch, at Ginsberg's proximity, at Ginsberg's patience, but he forced himself to focus on the donuts. Maybe the party *was* a terrible idea, and maybe he'd run screaming from this place the instant Ginsberg left his life, but he couldn't bear the thought of disappointing the kid while he was still here. And that meant a kick-ass party. Which apparently meant bacon donuts.

Ginsberg guided him to tip up the bowl and spoon in a bit of the dry ingredients at a time, running the mixer in between each addition. He kept *touching* Derrick—a hand on his forearm, fingers over Derrick's own, a palm resting warm and confident at the small of Derrick's back. Like he found a man baking sexy. Like it never even occurred to him that this wasn't the sort of work real men were supposed to do.

Derrick thought back to Ginsberg in that apron, cooking him breakfast. God, he'd been all man and then some that morning. Maybe it wasn't the cooking that was the problem. Maybe the problem was *Derrick.*

If he really was the problem, then it was a fatal flaw. Born and bred in him, and he hadn't changed for Jim who'd known him nearly all his life so how the hell would he be able to change for Ginsberg in the span of eight to twelve weeks? All the more reason for Ginsberg to get right back into his Hollywood production life with people who didn't have stupid hang-ups, who respected him and could keep up and didn't let dumb shit like baking make them insecure messes.

Hell, someone like Jim, maybe, who was currently sharing his juicy *Wolf's Landing* fan-theories and "head canons"—whatever the hell those were—in between teaching Ginsberg the optimum oil heat for frying donuts as well as walking him through the prep he'd need to do the morning of the party.

"We'll fry three up tonight just so you can see how it's done, but you definitely want to save frying the rest for sometime tomorrow so they're nice 'n fresh for the hipsters. Plus, the dough really should chill overnight. Just don't let Derrick anywhere near the hot oil tomorrow, 'kay? In fact maybe just put him on dishes until it's time to do the toppings."

Derrick thought to argue, defend his honor, but honestly Jim was probably right.

Jim gestured to his box of supplies. "There's recipes in there for maple, chocolate, and vanilla glazes, as well as sprinkles and the pink peppercorns, of course. The bacon, once it's out of the oven and cooled, you can just crumble and leave in the fridge. When you're ready to use it, just sprinkle it on some of the maple-glazed donuts. Sorry I can't be here tomorrow to help, but there's no way my boss is gonna stand for two sick days in a row." Derrick took a breath to say it was fine, but Jim just steamrolled on. He always had talked like it was going out of style. "Maybe if you do this again, we can graduate to Donut Making 102 and try some fillings! I've been dying to try my hand at my own jams and jellies. And you *know* a donut with powdered sugar is a one-way ticket to sucking each other's fingers!" He waggled his eyebrows at Derrick, who glared back. "*Any-who*." Jim popped his thumb in his mouth like he was sucking off his own powdered sugar, popped it out with an exaggerated kissing sound, and then winked at Ginsberg. "So how about it. Time to burn some donuts, hey?"

As it turned out, they *didn't* burn the donuts. Jim showed them how to cook the first one, and then Ginsberg and Derrick took a turn at donuts number two and three. They blotted the oil and topped them with a simple sugar glaze even Derrick was pretty sure he couldn't screw up, and then *finally* got to the good part: stuffing their faces.

The donuts were dense and cakey—"And that's why we let them chill and rise!" Jim chirped—but easily the best thing Derrick had so much as pretended to cook since he'd taken over this place. He was . . . actually kind of proud of himself? Surprised at how *good* it felt to be eating the fruits of his (admittedly very partial) labor without having to scrape off the burnt bits first or choke it down with coffee. It didn't hurt that Ginsberg kept grinning at Derrick over his own donut, either, like *he* was proud of Derrick too.

Derrick stopped midchew. Suddenly it wasn't his damn donut he was hungry for.

He was starting to appreciate the sentiment behind Jim's crude powdered sugar joke.

Especially watching Ginsberg delicately plucking hunks of soft, warm donut and popping them into his soft, waiting mouth.

He glared at the guy as he stuffed his own face, weirdly resentful.

So Ginsberg's entire existence seemed to disprove every-fucking-thing Derrick once believed about life and happiness and himself. But did he have to look so damn sexy while he was at it?

Did he have to be so damn charming that Derrick wished he could stick around and upend his life forever?

Except he wouldn't be sticking around. Even if he didn't have that exciting Hollywood career to go back to, what the hell did Derrick have to offer someone like Ginsberg?

Nothing. Which was why Derrick needed to put these feelings—whatever the hell they were—to bed.

They finished their donuts and followed them with a proper lunch before starting on their second, less supervised batch of donut batter. Derrick had gone quiet and sort of surly, though Ginsberg couldn't figure out why. Even their unrisen donuts had come out great, and Jim was a hoot and a half, and even Victoria was behaving, begging quietly by the table rather than yipping at their heels. Unfortunately, Ginsberg couldn't find any openings to ask what was bothering Derrick—not with Jim here, and honestly, not with his own growing concerns. That voice in his head that always—he squinted at his cast; well, okay, *almost* always—kept him safe. The one that was telling him Derrick was a giant moody grump because he was *in a kitchen* (gasp), because his peppercorns were *pink*, because there were no trees to chop or fires to light or animals to hunt while running a B&B, or whatever it was Derrick thought he needed to do to stop his dick from falling off.

But maybe, Ginsberg thought as he watched Derrick measure an eighth-teaspoon of salt so carefully you'd think he was making high explosives or something, he was being unfair to Derrick. Maybe this was just how Derrick reacted to change, or challenge, or both.

It was almost too bad Ginsberg couldn't stick around to find out. He had about eight million errands to run before the concert tomorrow, including a three o'clock meet-up with Tori to discuss any last-minute details.

"Well," Ginsberg announced when the mixer shut off. Was it his imagination, or did Derrick startle? They had been working in an unusually long stretch of quiet, he supposed, prepping endless batches of dough for tomorrow. "I have to head out. Errands to run, worlds to save, you know how it is."

Jim snorted a laugh, but Derrick only flashed him a sad little smile and knuckled at a spot of flour on his chin. "Escaping, huh?" Derrick laughed . . . ish. "All right. See you later."

"I should go too," Jim said before Ginsberg could respond. Maybe he was sensing the awkwardness, or maybe he'd just had enough of Derrick's Gloomy Gussing. "Remember: batter out of the fridge in the morning, *at least—*"

"Two hours to rise in a warm-but-not-hot place, I *know*." Wow, Derrick really had been paying attention? His exasperation faded into a soft smile, and he touched Jim's arm. "Thank you, Jim. For . . . you know." He rolled his head at the counter, the table, the fridge. "Everything. It, um." Another head roll. Derrick trying to express his feelings was starting to remind Ginsberg of a spooked horse. "It really means a lot to me that you, you know." Jim smiled patiently but didn't let him off the hook. "That you're still here after everything."

Jim grabbed him by both cheeks and plopped a big, noisy kiss in the center of his forehead. "Where else would I be, silly? *Someone's* got to make sure you don't burn this place down."

That was me*—literally—thank you very much*, Ginsberg thought, and then, *Holy crap, am I . . . jealous?*

What did he even have to be jealous *of*? Derrick talked about Jim like he was a living nightmare, when in fact he was sweet and giving and funny. And more than a little queeny, too, which made Derrick's inexplicable dislike of the guy pretty damning. Even if Ginsberg somehow had gotten himself an exception to Derrick's blanket prejudice toward men who weren't manly enough, that didn't make him feel any better about liking or being involved with a guy with that kind of prejudice in the first place.

On the other hand, Derrick had tried hard today. He'd kept more than one comment to himself, seemingly. He'd put a genuine effort into the donut making. And he'd thanked Jim for his help just as genuinely. Maybe he was learning. Not like it hadn't taken Ginsberg more than a few years to unlearn some seriously toxic gender shit, himself. Derrick just was starting later, that was all. He'd get there.

So that's how we're justifying our little crush, huh? He's trying? He'll get there? the cynical voice in Ginsberg's head taunted. *And I suppose we'll be the ones holding his hand the entire way, making excuses for him, putting up with his bullshit, all so we can justify wanting him to fuck us stupid?*

He had to get out of there, think with a clear head. He missed being on set every day, surrounded by people so comfortable in their own skin they could flaunt it on broadcast TV. He missed talking relationships with Carter. He missed his work. And maybe that was what all this . . . *whatever* it was with Derrick was about. He was just lonely and bored and looking for a new project.

Well thank God he had one that wasn't an effemiphobic lumberjack. Just . . . tangentially (okay, not so tangentially) related to an effemiphobic lumberjack. "So, uh," Ginsberg said as Derrick returned from walking Jim to the door. Bullshit chivalry or simple politeness? Hard to say. "I've got to head into town now, but I'll be back in time for dinner. You going to be okay here?"

Derrick surveyed the mess they'd made with a scowl and a sigh, but then he set his jaw and nodded once. "Yep. Who knows—maybe I'll even cook something edible."

"Better keep the fire extinguisher handy." The words slipped out of Ginsberg's mouth before he could censor their flirty lilt or the accompanying wink. He shouldn't be flirting with this guy—Derrick was a *disaster*. Way too big a project for Ginsberg's own mental health. Yet here he was.

And there *Derrick* was, laughing like Ginsberg had made a real joke instead of a gentle jibe. He checked his watch, the state of the kitchen, his watch again. Winked back. "Dinner at seven. Blackened . . . *everything*. Don't be late."

CHAPTER FOURTEEN

Two hours into his afternoon errands, Ginsberg came to a shocking realization: he was *rushing*. Not lingering to chat, not shooting the shit over a cup of coffee, not strolling through downtown, just one hurried chore to the next.

So he could get home. By seven.

To Derrick.

Shit.

This was not good. This was *so* not good. It was 4:30 and he only had one more stop to make before he could return to the B&B, and it occurred to him that in the back of his head he'd been planning what he'd do there for at least the last hour. Which bodywash to use—the jasmine and coconut butter, he thought; it left his skin so soft but didn't smell too "girly" for Derrick's sensibilities. Which products to put in his hair—just the leave-in conditioner that let him style it a bit but wouldn't make his hair crusty or sticky if a certain lumberjack were to run his fingers through it. Which outfit to wear—his fave distressed skinny jeans, to show off his butt (no he hadn't missed the way Derrick kept staring at it) and the tight V-neck tee he'd picked up at American Apparel a few years back that would make it crystal clear to Derrick there was no such thing as too pink for a real man.

When had he decided that they'd be getting close enough for Derrick to sniff him and touch his hair?

He hadn't, that's when. Though no denying that his dick was getting mighty interested in the prospect. He had to stop right there on the sidewalk and subtly adjust his packer to ease some pressure.

Nothing like a disaster you could see coming a mile away that you *still* walked headlong into. Though that *was* pretty much his job description, right?

You already broke your arm, idiot. Don't break your heart, too.

Well, they could still have a nice dinner together, couldn't they? To advance-celebrate their sure-to-be-successful party? Nothing said they *had* to get naked.

Okay, so maybe they'd get naked. But that didn't mean Ginsberg had to get his heart involved. Calculated risk, that was his whole business.

Still, better make one more stop before he went home.

Because oh boy was he going to need liquor for this.

Jarred pasta sauce. A box of dry spaghetti. He'd joked about lighting everything on fire, but he was self-aware enough to know that for him, unlike a lot of people, it wasn't just a joke. This shit was pathetic, but at least it was (mostly) un-screw-up-able. Right? *Right*?

Ginsberg would probably hate it. They ate fancy shit on film sets, didn't they? Kraft service or whatever it was called, catering in three meals a day like some high-end corporate retreat. Food with quinoa and kale and . . . What the fuck *was* quinoa even?

Whatever it was, Ginsberg probably hadn't eaten boxed noodles and canned sauce since he'd started *Wolf's Landing*, what, two years ago? Or was it three? God, how did he know so little about this kid when all he wanted to do was fuck him through the mattress and then tie him to it so he'd never leave again?

Whoa. Where did that *come from?*

He was just lonely, that was all. He missed his parents. *Desperately*, sometimes, never mind that he was a grown-ass man. He missed real work. Satisfying, hard, productive work. He even missed camp, all those burly-ass men with their feet kicked up around a fire ring, drinking beer and swapping stories.

He missed feeling useful. Wanted. Needed.

He plopped the entire jar of sauce into a saucepan and turned on the burner. Followed the directions on the jar: *Heat over low heat, stirring often, for 5 to 7 minutes, until hot. Optional: stir in 1 lb ground beef or sausage.*

He didn't have ground beef or sausage. Why hadn't he thought of that? There was a heap of crumbled bacon in the fridge, but that was for the donuts, and besides, did bacon even go with tomato sauce?

Bacon goes with everything, *darling.* He could practically hear Jim purring it in his ear.

Yeah, no. Best just to leave it alone. He turned the fire down as low as it would go, then filled another, larger pot with water for the spaghetti. Salted it according to the directions on the box, then set it to boil.

He realized five minutes later that the sauce was already hot, and the pasta was eight minutes from being done. He also realized he had no idea when Ginsberg was going to be home and it was only 5:30 and the only reason he could possibly have had to have started cooking something this simple this early was nerves.

Reheating it in the microwave later wasn't exactly going to help the meal's appeal. At least microwaving had a low likelihood of fire—just so long as he didn't put tinfoil in like that one time. Or accidentally leave a fork in the bowl like that other time.

The front door opened as he was testing a piece of pasta (still not done), and Victoria peeled out of the kitchen, yapping like she could make up for her size with sheer volume. *Shit.* He quickly killed the burners and took off after her—if that was a guest . . .

But no, it was just Ginsberg. Which, okay, yes, still a guest, but it wasn't like he hadn't seen the ugly side of the Bayview B&B already. Besides, Victoria actually seemed to like him. He put down his packages with a chuckle and bent to pet her as she jumped up on his shins, tail wagging wildly.

"You're home early," Derrick blurted. Never mind that it *wasn't* home to Ginsberg and never would be. He'd wanted to get the table set before Ginsberg came back. He'd even planned to look up which side of the plate the fork and knife and napkin went on. Too late now, though.

Ginsberg flushed, uncharacteristically bashful. "Yeah, uh, well, I guess . . . I guess I didn't have as much to get done this afternoon as I thought. Oh, and, Carter was busy. Hey, is that Italian I smell?

I uh—" He stooped to grab one of the bags at his feet, pulled out a bottle of wine. "I bought a nice Chianti. Lucky guess!"

Derrick knew less about wine than he did about running a B&B, but it was awfully sweet of the kid to spring for some, especially with his money troubles. Hopefully he hadn't paid more than ten bucks for it—you could get buzzed (or drunk?) just as easily on the cheap stuff as the pricey shit.

"Thanks." He took the bottle with one hand, waved vaguely toward the kitchen with the other. "It's not *really* Italian, I mean, I just sort of, you know. Heated up some sauce."

He felt ashamed to even say that, but it seemed more shameful to lie and try and pass it off as made from scratch.

"I understand if you don't wanna eat it. If you wanna order something in or whatever."

Derrick braced himself for the disappointment—and there was no denying it *was* disappointment he'd feel, even if it was just some shitty meal from a box and a jar—but Ginsberg only smiled and shook his head. Standing there surrounded by bags and a yappy dog and his good hand resting on his casted arm like maybe he'd overdone it today and it was hurting, and just *smiled*, pure and sweet as fresh fucking birch syrup. "Chianti doesn't go with takeout," he said. And then, "Do I have time to shower before dinner?"

The thought of Ginsberg dripping wet, in a towel, streaking down the hall with no shame at all made Derrick's blood rush south so fast he got light-headed. He had to clear his throat before he could manage, "Yeah, um, that'd be, that'd be fine. I'll, uh. Set the table. And let the wine, um. Breathe." That was a thing people did with wine, right? Ginsberg's nod made him pretty certain he hadn't screwed that up.

"Great. Be down in fifteen!"

Sadly (or not so sadly?) for Derrick, when Ginsberg arrived downstairs fifteen minutes later—actually twenty-two, but who was counting?—it wasn't dripping wet in nothing but a towel. On the plus side, it was in skintight jeans that showed off his athletic ass and a package Derrick very much wanted to see up close and personal, and an equally tight well-worn pink shirt with a deep V-neck that showed off his chest hair. His hair was damp and carefully combed, and . . . had he *styled* his facial hair?

Was Derrick *into* that?

Apparently so, according to Derrick Junior.

"You look," he said, "uh. Yeah. Dinner?"

Ginsberg grinned. "As long as there's wine."

Shit, he'd forgotten the wineglasses! He spun around and ran into the kitchen to grab them, then trotted back to the dining room. Which was neat and gleaming now because Ginsberg had helped him. Where Ginsberg was sitting now, frowning minutely at the plate before him. And why wouldn't he be? Derrick had made the damn meal and wasn't terribly interested in eating it.

But he sat down across the table from Ginsberg anyway, and plunked down the wineglasses, and remembered to put his napkin in his lap like a civilized human being while Ginsberg snatched up the wine bottle and poured a huge glass for each of them, then took a deep, deep drink out of his. Derrick might almost have called it a *chug*, except guys like Ginsberg didn't do things like that.

Guys who actually knew a single damn thing about wine.

Or who even *liked* wine. Not so much for Derrick, who had to use every ounce of willpower he had not to shudder at each sip of his glass. But Ginsberg had bought it special just for them, and he really didn't want to hurt Ginsberg's feelings or put his foot in his mouth any more than he had the last few weeks, so he sipped his wine in between bites of spaghetti and pretended both were good.

Ginsberg seemed to be doing the same. Either that or he was actually *enjoying* the food, though he *was* an actor—even if his face never showed on camera—and he could probably fake it with the best of them.

Of course, if he *was* faking it, then that meant he didn't want to hurt Derrick's feelings any more than Derrick wanted to hurt his.

And that was a good thing, right?

It sure felt good to sit across from him in his shiny new dining room with a passable plate of food in front of him while Ginsberg got progressively more chatty and cheerful as he drank.

And was that . . . was that the toe of Ginsberg's suede boot brushing Derrick's calf under the table?

Well, whatever was grazing him wasn't biting with tiny razor-sharp teeth, so it wasn't Victoria. Which meant it had to be Ginsberg. Which meant . . .

He stared across the table, to where Ginsberg was smiling at him from behind heavy-lidded eyes, absently twirling his fork in his spaghetti. Chin in his hand. Smiling. No, *biting his lower lip*.

Derrick trailed off midsentence, completely forgetting what they'd even been talking about a moment before. Something about tomorrow, maybe. Hard to focus on things like words when that foot was climbing past his knee and to the inside of his thigh. Christ, the kid hadn't even drained his first glass of wine yet. Which, admittedly, was a big glass, but still . . . He couldn't be *drunk*, could he?

If he weighs 150 pounds with his boots on, it's a lot. And is he still on pain meds for his arm? Have I ever seen him drink at all before?

The foot climbed higher, and Derrick totally did not let out a little squeak.

"You like me, don't you, Derrick?" Ginsberg asked with a smirk.

Derrick's hands curled into fists against the edge of the table, his back going ramrod straight. "Of course. You helped me keep my house from burning down. And you feed me way better food than this."

Ginsberg snorted. "That's not what I mean and you know it."

"I-I do?"

Ginsberg leaned forward, taking another gulp of his wine and licking the red off his lips obscenely. "I *mean* . . . You *like* like me, don't you, Derrick? As in, you want to fuck me."

Even though he'd been expecting something along those lines by Ginsberg's body language, Derrick still gaped at him, unable to respond. "I— You—"

"Don't you dare try and act flustered now, mister. Not after you pushed me into a wall half-naked."

Ginsberg's dark startled eyes and soft mouth, his body pressed to the wall but reaching out at the same time.

And then the realization of why they couldn't have this. That he'd be gone soon.

That nothing had changed between then and now. Not one thing.

Except, worse, now Ginsberg was tipsy at the very least. In any case, not thinking straight.

If this was a dream, then it was one of those stress dreams where Derrick was naked at the grocery store or chopping down endless trees that just popped up again like those inflatable punching clowns.

Derrick nudged Ginsberg's wandering foot away from his leg. "Fine. Yes. I do want to fuck you. But I'm not going to."

Ginsberg's face turned as red-purple as the wine he was drinking. He sank back in his seat.

"You've been drinking," Derrick explained, because the humiliation and rejection written all over Ginsberg's face was making something miserable twist in Derrick's gut.

Ginsberg scoffed. "I had one glass!"

Derrick scoffed right back at him. "Which is apparently one glass too many for a lightweight like you."

The hurt morphed into a challenging scowl. "Fine. So if I still want you to fuck me in the morning, you'll fuck me?"

Would he? Or was he using that glass of wine as a convenient excuse not to get too attached?

But really, since when had fucking a guy *ever* made him too attached? His partners had always been pretty casual. Except the one who wouldn't go away no matter how hard he tried, but Ginsberg wasn't Jim. He took another sip of too-sweet wine to buy himself one more moment—a moment terribly misused picturing a *sober* Ginsberg naked and writhing beneath him. He nearly choked before he managed to swallow. Gritted out, even though he knew it was a terrible idea, "Tomorrow."

"You're just putting me off," Ginsberg said. He frowned. Derrick would have accused him of sulking, if not for how genuine that frown seemed.

Something in Derrick's chest squeezed. "If I was just putting you off, would I do this?" He leaned across the table, grabbed Ginsberg by the nape of his neck, and pressed a firm kiss to his wine-stained mouth.

Ginsberg's arms were halfway up to cupping Derrick's head or tangling in his hair, but Derrick pulled back before those hands could touch him. Because if he let that happen, there'd be no waiting until tomorrow. And God knew Derrick was a big enough fuckup already; he had no intention of adding *taking advantage* to his list.

Ginsberg seemed pretty put out about it, sitting back with a pout on his flushed-pink face and then pouting some more as he poked at his shitty food. But it was better this way. Right? This way Ginsberg would still respect him in the morning.

And Derrick needed that. Needed it maybe even more than he could bear to admit.

CHAPTER FIFTEEN

Derrick peered out from the kitchen as Ginsberg greeted yet another clump of guests at the door. This place hadn't seen so many people since his parents had died—correction: this house had *never* seen so many people—and Derrick was man enough to admit that it was freaking him out.

But the band had set up, the sound checks had gone smoothly, the hipster playlist Ginsberg had put together was keeping everyone entertained until the real concert started, and the first several batches of donuts and drinks were being well received by the milling crowd. Which was milling *everywhere* while waiting for the band: the dining room, the living room, the family room, the front porch, even the hallways.

The espresso machine whirred and sputtered as it spat out a new round of drinks, all under the watchful eye of a scowling purple-haired teenager they'd borrowed from the Stomping Grounds. The kid was wearing a name tag on his apron that read, in black permanent marker scrawl: *PRONOUNS EY, EM, EIR.*

Not "his," stupid, "eir," Derrick reminded himself for the dozenth time as he put the coffees on a tray—complete with his mother's doilies—and carried it to the table in the family room where they'd set up the food. The place was starting to get so packed he had trouble making a path for himself, and it was with an uncomfortable mix of terror and excitement that he realized they were probably breaking fire codes right now.

Hipsters descended on the espressos before he could unload them off the tray, which he then used to carry dirty cups back to the kitchen.

He was running out of cups and the dishwasher could *not* keep up; they'd have to start washing them by hand soon.

Yay.

Back from door duty—no new arrivals in the last two minutes, thank God—Ginsberg was having a gay old time in Derrick's mother's apron, dropping donuts into hot oil and poking at them with tongs until they were ready to flip. He was humming along to the music as he cooked, swaying his hips to the beat. Even his casted arm was getting in on the action, and God, Derrick couldn't help but stare for a good long minute, imagining how it'd feel to be pressed up behind him, swaying along.

Even if he was wearing that frilly lacy apron.

Especially because he was wearing it?

Damn, the guy was definitely flicking some kinda switches in Derrick's head. Maybe it was that kiss they'd shared last night over dinner. The one Ginsberg seemed to have forgotten about completely—or at least hadn't said a word about the entire day. No way the kid had been too drunk to remember it after one big glass of wine, right? Especially since he'd woken up with no hangover this morning, if his behavior was anything to go on.

So why hadn't he said anything? Shouldn't a moment like that have *changed* things? If Derrick were in Ginsberg's shoes, he'd be embarrassed about his failed, semidrunk pass. He'd have a hard time looking Ginsberg in the eye now.

But Ginsberg just tonged the donuts from the oil to a plate of paper towels, humming and swaying and smiling whenever he caught Derrick's eye.

Maybe he was waiting for *Derrick* to say something. Being a fucking *gentleman.* After all, he had left the ball in Derrick's court, hadn't he? And maybe now he was just pretending everything was normal so as not to pressure Derrick.

Maybe they should talk.

Maybe I should just kiss him again.

He opened his mouth to do . . . well, one or the other of those things, he wasn't sure which, when a deafening screech of microphone feedback had them both clutching their ears. Well, Ginsberg clutched *one* ear. His broken wrist didn't bend right to cover the other.

Would it be weird or sweet if Derrick covered the other one for him?

No time to take a chance, because as suddenly as it had started, the horrible noise stopped. An amplified chuckle rang through the house. "Okay, okay. Technical difficulties I guess," a man's voice spoke from the common room. He introduced himself and the band. They played a few chords. No more feedback. Ginsberg looked up from the donuts he was dusting with cinnamon and sugar, stared out the archway of the kitchen like maybe he really wanted to be out there watching as well as listening.

Derrick glanced around the room—at the heaps and piles of mugs and plates to be cleaned, the trays of chilled dough waiting to be fried, the bowls of donut toppings and the floor covered in powdered sugar and pink peppercorns. Then back at Ginsberg, who'd been, frankly, a godsend the last two days, putting in more work than Derrick had any right to expect from *hired* help, let alone a volunteer. Then thought about all that was left to do—which, now that the band was firing up, wasn't nearly as much as before. People would be eating less, drinking less while they listened and danced.

Yeah, he could do this.

"Go on," he said.

Ginsberg blinked up at him from his nearly dusted tray of donuts. "Huh?"

"You want to be out there, I know you do. You've worked your tail off." He waved between himself and the purple-haired barista, who *was* getting paid to be here. "We've got this. Go. Have fun."

Ginsberg grinned so wide it nearly split his face in two, straightened up and wiped his hands on his apron. Funny how when Derrick thought of it that way—his—it stopped seeming girly at all, despite the frills. The kid crossed the distance between them, and leaned in, and it was an undeniable fucking magnetic pull that had Derrick leaning in too without even thinking. But Ginsberg just pecked him on the cheek, still grinning, then shook his head and grabbed the donut tray. "Nah," he said. "I'd rather listen with you. I'll just drop these off and be right back, yeah?"

Derrick blushed right to the tips of his ears. "Uh, y-yeah. Okay. I'll be, uh, here."

Making donuts.

With pink peppercorns.

For hipsters.

Just what in the flying fuck had his life even become?

Whatever it was, as terrified and overwhelmed as he felt, he was starting to think that maybe he loved it.

And, God help him, maybe that wasn't the only thing he was starting to love.

Partway through the night, in between the dishwashing and drying and the donut topping and the music, Ginsberg and Derrick found the time to just have fun together. The music wasn't particularly to Ginsberg's taste (and he was pretty sure Derrick didn't like it at all), and the heat of so many people and the sinks and the fryers was just this side of unbearable, but it seemed like neither of them could stop smiling. Or dancing. Or making flirty faces at each other every time Dean had eir back turned. And sometimes when Dean *didn't* have eir back turned, which always got them grossed-out looks but hell if either of them cared.

Fact was, Ginsberg couldn't stop thinking about the promise Derrick had made him at dinner last night. That he'd had no choice but to believe after their incredible kiss. That he knew he was going to collect on after the party, even though it was a terrible idea.

Like, really, just . . . *awful.*

Because Derrick was a *project*, and his therapist—and everyone else's mom, best friend, and tell-it-like-it-is coworker in the entire world, no doubt—had always said you can't change a man and trying will only get you hurt.

But he was a big boy. They both were. And a little sex couldn't hurt *that* much, could it? He just . . . had to make sure he didn't let his heart get involved.

Too late, genius. You know it is.

He scratched at the cast on his broken arm—didn't help, obviously, but scratching an itch was habit, instinct, and oh God maybe the universe was trying to tell him something here because if he let himself scratch *this* itch too, would it fail just as spectacularly?

Well, he was about to find out real soon, wasn't he? Because the clock was ticking toward eleven and then the band would stop and everyone would go home and it'd be just the two of them rattling around in this big old house, and Ginsberg's whole adult life had been about assessment and observation and proper reaction and he wasn't stupid—he knew exactly what his reaction was going to be once they were alone.

He wasn't sure he'd make it through even half that stack of dishes before he was climbing Derrick like a tree.

That glint in Derrick's eyes and the bulge in his Dickies pants told Ginsberg he wasn't the only one who might not make it.

The current song ended, and this time it wasn't followed by another. The crowd—nearly eighty people, amazingly enough, more than twice what they'd needed to pay for the band and the food and Dean's time—erupted into applause that went on and on and *on*. And on. And . . .

"And a special thanks to our hosts tonight, who made this whole thing possible: The Stomping Grounds of course, and The Bay—uh, Bayside? Bayview?—Bayview B&B, who provided this perfectly kitschy venue. Where are you, Bayview B&B guy?"

Derrick's hands froze on the plate he was scrubbing. Ginsberg half expected him to drop it. But instead he placed it carefully back in the sudsy water, turned to Ginsberg, and pointed vehemently with one wet finger. "You go," he half whispered, like he thought anyone could possibly overhear him all the way from the kitchen over the sounds of the crowd.

Ginsberg bit his lip against a teasing smile. "But I'm not the Bay-uh-Bayside-Bayview B&B guy."

"*Yes you are*!" Derrick whisper-shouted, jabbing his hand so hard at Ginsberg that some water droplets splashed him from three feet away. "This was *your* idea! All of it! Go!"

No holding back the grin now—was his big manly lumberjack *shy*?

"Together, then," he said. "C'mon. You deserve to know how well tonight went."

"Like I can't tell by this stack of dishes?" Derrick griped, but he dried his hands. "Okay. Fine. You're not going to let me off so, fine."

"Damn right I'm not. C'mon." He grabbed Derrick by the elbow, dragging him out through the dining room and to the living room. "Excuse me, pardon me!" he called. "Baysidebayview guy coming through!"

The crowd parted with a fresh round of applause. One guy saluted Derrick with his espresso, another with his donut. No mistaking the furious blush on Derrick's face, even in the low light, and damn if that didn't make Ginsberg even *more* desperate to get all these people out of here so he could have Derrick to himself.

The band pulled them both behind the microphones, underneath the spotlights they'd rigged up.

"Take a bow, guys!" the lead singer said, leading the applause, and Derrick gaped.

Luckily, Ginsberg was used to being the perfect supporting player. He grabbed Derrick by the hand, raised both their hands into the air, and then pulled them down into a full stage-style bow.

The crowd hooted and stomped and applauded.

Bowed as they were, and blinded by the lights besides, Ginsberg couldn't pin down Derrick's expression.

He didn't need to; he could tell how much this meant to Derrick by how Derrick squeezed his hand.

Even after the crowd had left, after the band had carted their instruments away and Derrick had locked the front door, he could scarcely believe he'd let Ginsberg drag him up on stage in front of all those people. Or that all those people had *cheered* him, thanked him, complimented him on the food and drink and decor as he saw them out. Some of them had even asked about availability, as if they actually thought they needed to worry about this place being booked full. As if they actually wanted to book here *at all.*

The common rooms looked like they'd been ransacked by a bear. The kitchen was worse. And there was still ticket money to count—and God did he ever *need* that money, but this event was more

Ginsberg's than his so there was no way he wasn't gonna make the kid take his share. He and Ginsberg really should be taking care of those chores right now, but instead they were lingering by the freshly shut front door together, staring into each other's eyes like a couple of lovesick puppies.

Or at least very, very *horny* ones.

"So—" Derrick said at the exact same time as Ginsberg. Somehow they managed to follow this with a mutual throat-clearing, and then a mutual "You first," like some kind of fucking comedy routine in a Hugh Grant movie.

"We should—" Derrick tried again, waving vaguely at the horrendous mess, when Ginsberg cut him right off at the knees with, "About that promise you made last night."

And speaking of Hugh Grant movies, enter the awkward sex talk. Derrick cleared his throat again, dropped his gaze to their feet: him in his old shit-kicking steel toes, Ginsberg in hand-painted baby-blue Converses. "Yeah, you're right, it was stupid. I shouldn't have kissed you while you were tipsy. Or talked to you that way. But if you're willing to put it behind you, I'm willing to—"

Put it behind me too, he thought, bewildered, as Ginsberg grabbed him by the lapels of his flannel shirt, shoved him up against the door with surprising force, and laid one square on his lips.

Or that. Derrick growled deep, clasping at Ginsberg's upper arms as he leaned in, licking into Ginsberg's mouth like a man who hadn't just been justifying why they shouldn't do any of this.

Ginsberg tasted like espresso and cinnamon-sugar, and his cast was digging hard into Derrick's chest, and *something* was digging just as hard into Derrick's hip and never in his entire life had he needed to get everybody's clothes off more than he did *right fucking now.* By the time his mind caught up with his body, he'd scooped Ginsberg into his arms and carried him down the hall and halfway across the kitchen.

"Where are you—" Ginsberg gasped out, but Derrick just spun them both around and used his back to shove through the door that led from the kitchen to his own private living suite.

"Bed," he grunted. Kid was heavier than he looked, all long lean muscle.

Ginsberg threw his arms around Derrick's neck—that fucking cast was shaping up to be mighty inconvenient—levered himself up a little in Derrick's arms and licked a stripe across Derrick's jaw and cheek. "Yes," he rumbled in Derrick's ear, then licked that too.

He hoped Ginsberg would be open to licking him some other places as well. And to *being* licked. Because holy Christ did he have plans.

He rushed through his living room, into the bedroom, and half dropped, half tossed Ginsberg onto the queen-sized bed. Ginsberg landed like a beetle on its back, chin and knees tucked in, good arm straight out to slap the mattress: same way they taught loggers to take a fall if they couldn't crouch and roll, but about fifty times more graceful and with entirely more laughing than swearing. He splayed out spread-eagle, caught Derrick's gaze, licked his lips and drawled, "Take me, mountain man."

Fuck. Didn't need to tell him twice. He stripped down to nothing but his socks in about zero point four seconds. Pounced. Straddled Ginsberg's thighs.

Ginsberg sat up just long enough to let Derrick tug his shirt over his head, then flopped back to the bed. Derrick let himself just *stare* for a minute, revel in the show he'd been too embarrassed to enjoy in the hallway that first morning. His balls were pressed hot and heavy to Ginsberg's left thigh, and it was all he could do not to grind on the kid like an animal, not to ravage every inch of skin with his tongue and fingers and teeth. But he didn't want it to be like that. Didn't want to blow too soon. Didn't want to make Ginsberg feel . . . *disposable.*

"Derrick?" Ginsberg asked, and only when Derrick tore his eyes away from that glorious body to meet his eyes did he realize that Ginsberg seemed . . . nervous. The kid hadn't possessed a single ounce of insecurity back in that hallway, so why—

Because now he knows you want him, and you're staring like an idiot instead of touching, and he's probably worried you think he's a freak.

"Can I . . ." Derrick's voice cracked as he moved his hands over Ginsberg's chest, the scar from his . . . what had he called it? Top surgery? . . . the mouthwatering line of hair that ran from his navel to beneath the waist of his skinny jeans. Ginsberg blinked up at him, waiting for him to finish a fucking sentence. "God, you're so . . ." He huffed, frustrated, too aroused, terrified of fucking this up. "I wanna cover you in candied bacon and eat you whole," he tried, and Ginsberg laughed, and *Derrick* laughed, and then hands were pulling him down by the neck and they were kissing and kissing, Ginsberg's sprinkling of chest hair prickling across his nipples, Ginsberg's five o'clock shadow rasping across his own. Derrick ground his cock against Ginsberg's denim-covered thigh, felt Ginsberg's own hips rocking up against his belly. Half wanted to kiss the kid *forever* but there were so many more pressing urges right now . . .

He pulled back, sat up, panting and flushed, lips tingling. Made himself slow the fuck down for a second. Let his hands explore this time, wondering where the line was between you're-hot-as-hell-and-I-can't-get-enough-of-you and gawking-because-you're-different. Because Derrick was sure as hell in the first camp, but what if Ginsberg read him as the other thing? Should he touch Ginsberg's chest? His groin? Ginsberg had seemed proud of his chest scars, but what if he was insecure about them with sex partners?

"You're making it weird," Ginsberg singsonged, smiling up at him, that expression like he was about to laugh or cover Derrick's face in puppy kisses, letting Derrick know it was all okay.

It was all okay.

Inspiration struck, and the first thing he touched was Ginsberg's good hand. Wrist, actually, which he dragged gently down to his own cock. Ginsberg caught a clue awfully quickly, curled his fingers around Derrick's shaft.

"You feel that?" Derrick growled, and thrust up once into Ginsberg's too-loose fist. "You feel what you do to me?"

Ginsberg's grin was downright cheeky, his fingers stubbornly teasing. "I've been watching what I do to you all evening. Question is, mountain man, what are *you* gonna do to *me*?" Then he let go of Derrick's cock altogether, threw his arm back out to the side.

"Watch your sweet little mouth, city boy," Derrick replied, fingers sliding against the grain through his treasure trail, up past his belly button and to Ginsberg's nipples.

"Or what?" Ginsberg gasped at the first light touch, bared his teeth. "You gonna put your dick in there?"

"Something like that, smart-ass."

"Not gonna lie, man. Not exactly a deterrent, over here."

"When I'm good and ready," Derrick said, and flicked his thumbs over Ginsberg's nipples again, harder this time. "Like that?" he asked—unnecessarily—when Ginsberg gasped and arched into his hands.

"Fuck yeah," Ginsberg breathed.

Derrick replaced his right hand with his mouth, traced his fingers over Ginsberg's scar instead. Ginsberg squirmed beneath him, and he had to shift to take some pressure off his dick before all those movements set him off too early.

"Tickles, man," Ginsberg said, lifting a hand at last, but only to nudge Derrick's from his scar to the button of his jeans. "I can't feel much there, but it's all like a giant tease." He cleared his throat pointedly, his hand making urgent little taps on the one Derrick now had over Ginsberg's fly.

Hey, never let it be said that Derrick couldn't take a hint. He inched down Ginsberg's body, back to that treasure trail again, this time following it with his lips and nose, breathing in the heady masculine scent that carried through the cloying smell of fried sweet batter. When he reached the waist of Ginsberg's jeans, he undid the button and zipper—no teasing, he was as eager as Ginsberg was—and worked jeans and briefs together down Ginsberg's thighs, where Ginsberg kicked them the rest of the way off.

He honestly hadn't known what to expect, hadn't even cared, really, because there was no way what was in Ginsberg's pants wouldn't be as hot as the rest of him just by dint of being *Ginsberg's*. He did have to admit to a moment of surprise, though, when he uncovered a cock and balls that looked so natural he actually marveled for a moment at how good doctors were at their jobs. But then he noticed the subtle difference in skin tones, the fact that Ginsberg's dick was attached with surgical tape instead of sinew. Who fucking cared, really, because his mouth was watering at the sight of it—it *was* a gorgeous cock, even if it was made of silicone. Was he supposed to treat it like Ginsberg could feel it? Take it off? Something else?

Ginsberg came to the rescue by stroking the top of his head and saying, "That's my packer. I could fuck you with it if you want; it even gets hard, with the right equipment. But I have to admit, I'm in the mood to *be* fucked tonight."

Derrick found himself nuzzling up against it, in the space between Ginsberg's packer and thigh. It was body-warm, and he kind of liked the way it felt, even gave in to the urge to flick his tongue out and taste it. Ginsberg splayed his thighs and let him, hand still resting gently in his hair. Humming with pleasure as Derrick gave the soft, smooth silicone a taste. Different, but good. He could totally get used to this.

If this was what Ginsberg wanted him to get used to, that was.

Derrick propped himself on his elbows between Ginsberg's legs, ran his hands up strong, hairy thighs. "Do I . . ."

"How about you untape it," Ginsberg asked, "and suck my *real* cock?" It was a teasing order, but even Derrick, dense as he could be, didn't miss the hint of nervousness behind it. "I mean, it's not . . . it's *different*, you know, but I—"

"It's perfect, I'm sure. Just like the rest of you." He worked carefully at the tape, not wanting to hurt Ginsberg or rip hairs out—and fuck was the guy hairy down there, nothing like the waxed metrosexual city boy Derrick had initially pinned him as. In fact, maybe Derrick wasn't the mountain man in this arrangement after all.

He fucking loved it.

Just as much as he loved what he found when he pulled the packer off and laid it aside.

Ginsberg's real cock, unlike his soft, flaccid packer, was as hard as Derrick's. Maybe a third the size, without the slit or heavy hanging balls he was used to seeing but otherwise surprisingly familiar territory. The head was even shaped like his own.

He wasted no time stuffing the whole thing in his mouth.

Ginsberg's fingers clenched tight in his hair, and he gritted out, "*Fuck*, dude!" and bucked up against him, hands holding his head in place. Derrick had always loved sucking cock but hated being choked on a dick—never had figured out how to stop his gag reflex—so his first instinct was to tense at Ginsberg's actions. But he realized half a second later that he *wasn't* choking, that Ginsberg *could* fuck his mouth without trouble. Oh man, this was . . . this was a match made in Heaven.

"Gonna make you blow so hard," he mumbled around Ginsberg's cock, a hand on Ginsberg's hip bone as he flicked his tongue along the underside. This was normally when he'd start playing with his lover's balls, too, but just because Ginsberg didn't have any didn't mean he couldn't rub two fingers along Ginsberg's taint while he curled his tongue around the cock in his mouth and sucked, burrowing in so close that Ginsberg's wiry hair tickled his nose.

"Mmm," Ginsberg hummed, and then, "Fun fact: I can multiple orgasm."

Christ. He slid his fingers from Ginsberg's taint back to his ass, rubbed at the hole without pushing inside. "Is that a challenge?"

"*Mmm,*" Ginsberg hummed again, grinding his ass down against Derrick's fingers. "Don't be shy about penetration."

Derrick grinned, practically *preening* at how quickly Ginsberg's nervousness had fled, how thoroughly he'd put the kid at ease. He brought his hand up to Ginsberg's mouth, slid his fingers past those soft plush lips, let Ginsberg get him nice and wet since Derrick's own mouth was still very occupied with Ginsberg's cock.

He was about to stuff his spit-wet index finger into Ginsberg's obviously hungry ass when the idea struck him. He pulled off Ginsberg's dick. "When you say don't be shy . . ." he prompted, rubbing in circles with his finger as his thumb drifted upward, right up to where Ginsberg's taint turned into something else.

Ginsberg propped himself up on his good elbow, wetting his lower lip with his tongue. Derrick was about to back off without another word when suddenly the corner of Ginsberg's mouth twitched upward. "Why Derrick!" he teased, and it was hard not to be a little annoyed that he was able to still sass when Derrick could barely string three words together. "Are you suggesting you'd like to give my bonus hole a bit of love?"

Bonus . . . Derrick's horny-stupid brain echoed, barely processing. *Bonus . . . bonus . . .*

"Because the answer is *fuck* yes. Knock yourself out, man. I'm down." With a grin, he flopped back onto the bed, making a show of spreading his legs nice and wide. His dick, fat and hard, was just begging for Derrick to get back to work, so he did. With a blow of air and a flick of his tongue, he fell back in, sucking Ginsberg in firm, unrelenting pulses as his hand burrowed between Ginsberg's legs.

His finger and thumb were still just wet enough as he spread them apart and teased one at each hole, slid them inside. He'd never touched a . . . a *bonus hole* before but it didn't seem so different from what he was used to, hot and giving and deep, with a little rough nub inside that made Ginsberg squirm and swear and moan when he rubbed at it. Oh yeah, G-spot—he focused on that for a bit, increasing the pressure as his mouth stayed busy on Ginsberg's cock, until Ginsberg's legs came up around his chest and locked tight behind his back, and Ginsberg's breathy little moans turned into an ongoing stream of *Oh yes* and *God* and *Right there, Derrick* and *Don't stop please don't stop* and then, finally, *OhgodI'mgonna—!* and then Ginsberg's fingers clenched painfully tight in his hair and Ginsberg's legs clamped the breath right out of his lungs as the muscles inside Ginsberg spasmed around Derrick's fingers.

Stupid and lust-crazed as he was, it took him a moment to realize Ginsberg had just orgasmed dry—which, wow, *really* kind of nice not to get a load of bitter, salty cum that your partner inevitably got insulted about if you didn't swallow.

He sat up, licking the heady taste of Ginsberg on his lips, thumb and finger still stroking slowly in and out of Ginsberg's body as the kid came down from his ride—a knock-him-out wild one by the boneless, stupefied expression on his face. This was normally the point at which he'd expect his partner to fall asleep—or lazily return the favor while fighting off sleep—but Ginsberg was both fucked stupid and alert—a fact Derrick Junior was *very* glad of—and biting his fucking lip again, damn him.

"Round two?" Ginsberg asked, reaching out to grab Derrick's cock. No teasing this time; his fingers closed tight and made firm, decisive strokes while Derrick knelt above him shamelessly losing his mind. Ginsberg patted Derrick's hip with his casted hand—the other hand still blissfully busy—and said, "Up," and Derrick obeyed with what little cognition remained to him. Unfortunately, once he'd risen up on his knees, Ginsberg let go of his dick. Fortunately, Ginsberg took the opportunity to roll over onto his stomach, tucking a pillow under his hips and lifting his ass up nice and high.

"Hope you got a condom in here," Ginsberg said, wiggling his ass at Derrick, and that had to be just the *sassiest* fucking ass-wiggle he'd ever seen in his life.

Finest ass he'd ever seen in his life, too. Could bounce a quarter off that fucking thing, except for all the hair. Derrick scritched his fingers through it, then drew the cheeks apart. "Yeah, I got a condom." Then added, "When I'm good and ready," because as hard and aching and eager to fuck Ginsberg as he was, he *still* had other plans first.

"When I'm good and ready, he says!" Ginsberg teased. "Don't even pretend you're still in charge he—eere!" The word had turned into a squeal midway, because Derrick had lunged forward, lapping with long, strong strokes of his tongue across Ginsberg's asshole.

Now this he was an old hand at.

All-time world ass-eating champion, that was what Jim had called him.

Why the hell was he thinking of *Jim* at a time like this?

Talk about a boner killer, but luckily for Derrick Junior, Ginsberg's bubble butt was hot enough to counteract the effect. Derrick could happily bury his face in it all night long. And from the sounds Ginsberg was making, he'd be just as happy for Derrick to stay there.

Ginsberg had already come once, and seemed well on his way to orgasm #2, while Derrick was pretty sure his own nuts were starting to resemble Smurfs, so it was strange how content he felt, how *happy*, how little desire he had to take his turn before he got Ginsberg off again. It'd never been like that with Jim. It'd never been like that with, well, *anyone*. And just what the fuck did it mean that it was like that now?

Probably best not to think too hard on it. After all, Ginsberg wouldn't be in that cast forever. Wouldn't be *here* forever. Just... enjoy it while it lasted, that was all.

Derrick's tongue licked and curled and darted around and inside Ginsberg's ass, and Ginsberg was moaning and squirming more than ever, but it was harder to get lost in it now that Derrick had made the mistake of thinking about *later*. At least Ginsberg, with his head buried in his good arm, didn't seem to notice the difference. Just kept making those noises and grinding his hips into the pillow beneath them, and then finally breaking down and begging, "Jesus, Derrick, *fuck* me already."

Happily.

He sat up, reached for the condoms and lube in his bedside drawer. Ginsberg's hole was sloppy wet and nice and loose from all that attention, but a little extra slick never hurt anyone.

Ginsberg propped himself on his good arm and turned his head to watch Derrick roll the condom on his cock. Derrick was so achingly hard and edged out he had to be careful how much he touched himself putting on the rubber; no way was he gonna ruin things by coming in his own hand like some eager teen. Ginsberg's face was flushed, pupils blown, lips parted *just so*—a perfect fucking Hollywood picture of decadence and lust and need. Derrick felt huge and clumsy by comparison, lube leaking through his fingers as he squeezed the bottle too hard, hands shaking as he parted Ginsberg's cheeks with one and stuffed two fingers inside him with the other.

Ginsberg shuddered and groaned, humping his pillow. "C'mon," he moaned, needy. "C'mon, c'mon."

Derrick added another finger. "*Believe* me, I'm hurrying. I don't wanna—"

"I'm a stuntman, Derrick," Ginsberg said, turning his head to meet Derrick's eyes again. "We're all crazy. I *like* a little pain."

Oh God. Derrick had his fingers out of Ginsberg's ass and his cock in it so fast he didn't even remember making the switch. It was all just heat and slick and tightness, perfect pleasure shooting from his dick to his balls and straight up his spine as Ginsberg moaned "*Fuck* yes" beneath him and buried his head back in his arm.

Derrick took the encouragement and ran with it—or rather *thrust* with it—never so thankful for a condom as he was right now; without the layer of latex to dull the edges of the ecstasy, he'd be gone in thirty seconds. As it was, he bent forward over Ginsberg's raised ass, draped himself across that muscled back and buried his face in Ginsberg's neck. Inhaled deeply, then let his lips and tongue wander where they would. The angle forced his hips to slow, but neither of them seemed to mind that at all. Ginsberg just twisted his head around to crush his mouth against Derrick's—an even more awkward angle, from the looks of it—then murmured against Derrick's lips, "Touch me, please."

It took Derrick a second to figure out what he was asking for—he *was* touching him, all the fuck over, in fact—but once it clicked he wormed a hand between Ginsberg's hips and the pillow, feeling along all that slippery, sweaty flesh until he found Ginsberg's hard little cock, grasped it with his thumb and two fingertips and jerked him in short, quick bursts. Then quicker, harder—he *really* needed Ginsberg to come soon or it wasn't gonna happen with him still inside the kid, and he wanted that, like some sappy fucking romance novel he *wanted* them to go over the edge together, and it seemed kind of strange that Ginsberg *was* taking so long considering all the foreplay and attention he'd lavished on the kid, until he realized . . .

Ginsberg didn't *have* a prostate.

Had he . . . had he been fucking the wrong hole the entire time? Should he have been aiming for the G-spot instead?

Not that Ginsberg was complaining, but still . . . Derrick drew up for a moment, pausing to catch his breath and pull himself back from that teetering edge. Ginsberg immediately looked over his shoulder again, expression curious and teasing.

"Tired, old man?" he asked.

"No, I—" *Old?* Little brat. "I just, I mean . . ." He shifted his weight onto one hand, gestured vaguely with the other—the one he'd been jacking Ginsberg with. Even through the sweat and exertion and arousal, he could feel his cheeks heating. *Oh, fuck it. Just spit it out.* "AmIfuckingtherighthole?"

"Oh. My. God. Oh my God! Derrick!"

Was he . . . was he *laughing*?

"Derrick honey," Ginsberg squeaked, the muscles in his ass clenching hard and sweet around Derrick's cock. Derrick couldn't help it; he rolled his hips, thrust in slow. "Why would you think there *is* a wrong hole, even?"

Derrick stilled, trying to process an answer to the question while having the sense squeezed out of him. "Because . . . because. You know. You don't have—"

"You think I need one? Wasn't necessary when you were rimming me, was it?"

"No, but—"

"And my anatomy may be different, but there's plenty of parts in there for a nice big cock to rub up against and get me excited, you feel me?"

Ginsberg squeezed his muscles again for emphasis, and Derrick barely managed to choke out a "Yes."

Ginsberg grinned, teasing again. "Good. So get back to that hammering, mountain man; you've got a job to finish."

"Yes sir, Mr. Hollywood," Derrick growled, and did as he'd been told.

Derrick's dick inside him felt just as good as Ginsberg had hoped. Like a fucking iron rod, solid and heavy and unyielding.

But Derrick didn't just meet Ginsberg's expectations, he exceeded them. Never in a million years had Ginsberg expected a gay man to volunteer to play with his original plumbing. It had always hurt to be . . . overlooked like that, but he made himself accept it.

With Derrick, he didn't have to.

The guy had proven himself a sensitive and considerate lover, not that Ginsberg would ever say that aloud.

Not that he even *could* say anything, what with Derrick's dick pounding the air out of his lungs.

So instead, he just rolled his hips and clung to the bedsheets and thrust his cock into Derrick's surprisingly dexterous fingers, chasing after an orgasm that seemed just beyond his grasp. Well, no surprise there. For all he'd bragged to Derrick, the second climax was always trickier than the first.

Tricky, but not impossible, especially not with Derrick filling him so deeply, his pace turning brutal as he got closer to his own release. And it was that—that relentless pounding driving him forward across the mattress and accompanied by increasingly rough handling of his dick—that pushed him past the breaking point, had him clenching and tensing and—fuck, shit, he always did this—*laughing* as his orgasm short-circuited every nerve in his body, leaving him out of control, trembling and twitching as Derrick thrust deep and went still, burying his scratchy face in Ginsberg's neck and shoulder as he came.

Derrick stayed in place for several long moments, unmoving except to feather little kisses across Ginsberg's shoulder and neck. He was damp and hot and heavy atop Ginsberg, but it wasn't like Ginsberg wasn't used to being at the bottom of a pile of bodies (granted, usually not naked), and besides, he actually liked the press of it, the firmness and the sense of security it brought. He'd never have pegged Derrick for cuddly, but he of all people should've known how deceiving looks could be.

And he'd have been happy to stay like that awhile, he really would've, but it turned out that plaster casts were a terrible inconvenience in these sorts of situations. His arm was itchy and aching, and the top of the cast was biting into his muscle, and Derrick's weight wasn't helping.

But oh, the feel of Derrick going soft inside him was almost, *almost* incentive enough to grin and bear it.

"Um," he finally said. Wiggled his butt because words were surprisingly hard to come by just now. He was still tingling everywhere, winded like he'd just shot an unusually strenuous fight sequence in a single long take. "Heavy."

"R-right," Derrick muttered. "Nothing lasts forever, huh?" He rolled off of Ginsberg and right out of bed, the base of his condom clutched to his flaccid dick.

"Nothing that cuts off my circulation, anyway," Ginsberg teased, rolling onto his back as Derrick waddled to the bathroom, giving Ginsberg a lovely view of that tight fuzzy lumberjack butt.

He basked in the afterglow as he listened to water running in the bathroom. Not just the afterglow of the sex, as amazing as it'd been, as amazing as *Derrick* had been about . . . well, everything. No, it was more than that. The party, the cooking, the way he'd *tried* so damn hard, how much fun they'd ended up having, how shy he'd been taking his bow at the end of the night . . .

Ginsberg hated to admit it, but he was maybe kind of really pretty sure he might be, just a little, starting to fall in love.

And then Derrick came out of the bathroom with a warm washcloth and crawled between Ginsberg's legs with a wicked smile and wiped the lube and the sweat away and followed it with more of those little feather kisses all around his thighs and butt and pubes, and Ginsberg got to worrying he might be starting to fall in love more like a lot.

Well, worse things had certainly been known to happen, right?

CHAPTER SIXTEEN

Ginsberg woke up in the morning tangled in a mass of heavy limbs, a smile on his face and that same sweet swell of emotion in his chest.

And to a ringing phone. Not his, Derrick's. He fumbled around for it anyway, but there really was no escaping Derrick's whole octopus thing until finally the man rolled over on his own, smacking at the nightstand on his side of the bed until his fingers connected with the handset.

"'lo?" he mumbled.

A beat where Derrick just listened. Ginsberg couldn't hear who was on the other end of the line, but whoever it was made Derrick sit up, dig a pen and paper out of the nightstand drawer. "Yes, of course, absolutely. No, short notice isn't any problem at all. No, neither is early check-in. Ten is great, yeah, no problem." He scribbled something on the pad Ginsberg couldn't read. A date, he thought. A name.

"Yes. Yes, great. We'll see you then. Thank you."

He hung up the phone almost in slow motion, then turned to Ginsberg with a lopsided grin, held up the paper like a trophy, and said, "Ha! Paying customer!"

"Fuck yeah!" Ginsberg cried, and broken arm be damned, he launched himself on top of Derrick, peppering his face with kisses.

They didn't leave his bed until after noon.

The phone rang twice more before dinner, and both times it was people calling to book. After dinner, they finished tidying the mess the concert had made, then celebrated their new victories with a bottle of wine and a fire, which inevitably led to sex on the rug in front of the fireplace. The first guests were arriving in the morning, so they played at responsible adulthood and went to bed early to sleep off all the liquor and orgasms. And when the couple—a pair of midthirties hipsters with more camera equipment than Ginsberg had ever seen off a set—checked in, Ginsberg smiled at them from behind the counter and elbowed Derrick until he remembered to offer to carry their bags upstairs. Even Victoria, who Derrick had long insisted was too poorly behaved to keep around guests, only gave a few friendly yips and sniffs and then went back to Derrick's rooms.

As they gave the guests the grand tour, it occurred to Ginsberg that there were no photos of the rooms on the B&B website, so he resolved to fix that just as soon as they'd gotten the hipsters settled.

While Ginsberg spent the afternoon Instagramming the place inside and out, Derrick spent it chopping wood—lots of extra people coming to use it this week—and vocally freaking out over what to serve for breakfast tomorrow.

It was Ginsberg who suggested the possibility of paying Jim to bake some pastries to serve with their gourmet coffee and fresh fruit, avoiding the minefield of over-easy eggs and crispy bacon entirely. The pastries would be a great draw, and would buy enough time for Ginsberg and Derrick to practice egg and bacon and hash brown cooking until Derrick had it down.

Then, who knew—maybe they could even graduate to frittatas and pancakes and the like.

But one step at a time. Fortunately, Derrick was relieved to pass off the responsibility to Jim, and Jim was squee-inducingly excited that a) Derrick had customers, and b) Derrick wanted to feed said customers his pastries. He bustled in at 5:30 the next morning with enough pastries to feed twenty people rather than two, and refused to accept anything more than a ten-dollar bill for his trouble. He stuck around a few extra minutes to ply Victoria with affection, kiss a sleep-grumpy Derrick on the cheek, and kiss Ginsberg on *both* cheeks, and then he bustled off to work.

The hipsters went nuts over the pastries. Chocolate-filled croissants, teeny little fruit tarts with fresh berries, mini muffins in four flavors, and—of course—bacon maple-glazed donuts.

They decided to stay an extra day.

And apparently they told all their friends—that, or the photos Ginsberg posted had started working their magic—because by the end of the week, the B&B was half-full, with reservations stretching into the spring. Jim was stopping by every morning, and Derrick had, in his own words, "manned up" and learned to make eggs in several styles, plus bacon, sausage, and hash browns that didn't set the kitchen on fire. All told, they were chopping a lot of wood, washing a lot of sheets and towels, cleaning a lot of rooms, cooking a lot of meals (by the end of the second week, they were crowded enough to justify the effort of serving afternoon tea with Jim's leftover pastries), and—best part—having frankly ridiculous quantities of celebratory sex.

Derrick seemed very happy, in the rare moments when he wasn't too busy to think about his feelings. But Ginsberg . . . was getting bored.

His cast itched all the damn time. He was sick of having to sit out work that required two arms. There was a lot to be done, but other than washing dishes and toilets, Derrick seemed to have them in hand. Carter had called and told him they'd settled on a new guy to do the stunts Ginsberg was missing.

"But he doesn't understand the way to move," Carter complained, sounding sorry as hell to be doing it no matter how kindly he was phrasing things. "It doesn't blend. It's not *seamless* the way it is for you and me. Please, please, can you come in and give him some pointers? You know, watch some of his footage, tell him how to be more . . . me? Natalya's got the whole stable of stuntmen to worry about, and I'd do it myself but apparently I'm not that much of an expert on my own physicality."

"Well, you can hardly study yourself the way I've studied you," Ginsberg said, waving to Derrick as he shouldered his way through the door with a big basket of laundry in hand.

"It's kind of sexy when you put it that way. Can I steal that?" Carter asked.

"Uh, sure, if you find an opportunity, I guess!" Ginsberg laughed, then mouthed *Carter Samuels* to Derrick.

Who? Derrick mouthed back. He set the basket of laundry onto the coffee table and plopped down on the couch, getting right into folding.

Wolf's Landing *guy*, Ginsberg replied.

"Anyway, I already talked to Natalya, and she's totally cool with it, and even Finn conceded he'd be willing to pay you to come consult for a few days. I mean, we're stuck with this guy until you come back, and he wants it to be right, you know?"

"I dunno, man, are you *sure* Natalya's not going to object to me coaching her stuntman?"

"Promise. It'll be easy work. Your agent will take care of all the details, just . . . please come in? *Please*?"

Ginsberg looked to the heaping basket of laundry Derrick was folding, to the small crease between Derrick's brow that hadn't been there a minute ago, to his stupid itchy casted arm, and then to the ceiling as he flopped back on the couch. He was bored anyway, wasn't he? And not very useful here after all? "Yeah, okay. Should be fine. Tomorrow?"

Derrick's nostrils flared. He sighed, then smiled wearily, picking up a fitted sheet and folding it like a damn expert.

"Yeah, 8 a.m. call."

That meant Ginsberg wouldn't be able to help with breakfast tomorrow. Considering rush-hour traffic, he'd have to be up and out of here by 7:15 at the absolute latest, maybe even seven if he didn't want to risk rolling in late on his first day back to work in over a month. Not that he'd be holding up the filming or anything, but still, professionals respected the rehearsal process and everyone's time.

Also, Natalya kind of scared the crap out of him.

In a good way, of course—he liked her plenty—but still.

"So, um." He smiled at Derrick, who was folding sheets with unnecessary quantities of concentration. "That was work. Apparently they're having some trouble with my replacement and wanted to know if I could come in and coach him a bit."

"Sounds like you're irreplaceable," Derrick said with a pathetic little smile.

"So are you," Ginsberg replied, leaned in, and kissed him. "Need help with the sheets?"

"Nah. 'Bout time I learned to do things around here on my own. Considering."

It's just a few days' work, he wanted to protest, but that wasn't really true, was it. Maybe now it was a few days' work, but in two weeks this cast was going to come off, damn it, and when it did, he'd be resuming his full-time duties. Or at least, after some PT, probably. He doubted Carter would stay quiet if they tried to let him go for good. Which meant that in six, maybe eight weeks, he'd have to start working long days again, crazy hours, sometimes in the middle of the night, sometimes Fraturdays, and often right through breakfast. Which meant that Derrick really *would* have to learn how to run this place by himself.

Which, to be fair . . . it *was* Derrick's place. Not *theirs*, just Derrick's. No matter how much time they'd spent working on it together or how close they'd become or how much closer still they might yet become.

"I'm glad to hear that, because I'm afraid I'll have to miss breakfast tomorrow, unless all the guests are down here by six." Which was never going to happen.

"S'okay," Derrick said to the sheet he was folding. "I got the staples down pat, and Jim'll be by like always with the fancy shit."

Ginsberg was relieved Derrick didn't seem angry about him ducking out of his duties. After all, he had been living here rent-free for two weeks now; Derrick had refused the second month's rent in light of the help he'd provided. And as for Jim's contributions . . . "You need to start paying him a wage or something. Like actually *hire* him, so he can stop stuffing the cash you give him between your couch cushions."

"Is *that* where that money's coming from? I thought we had some kind of moneybags brownie creeping in at night."

"Sorry, man. The only Brownie in this place is yours truly. Wanna buy some cookies?"

"Huh? Is that a, uh . . . Hollywood thing?"

"Is that your not-wanting-to-piss-me-off way of saying 'silly city boy'? Adorable. And no. You know how in Scouts there's Cub Scouts and Boy Scouts depending on your age group? Well in Girl Scouts they've got Brownies when you're little. And you sell cookies. And I was one. Still know the oath!" He held up two fingers in illustration.

Derrick shook his head. "I totally never even thought you wouldn't have been in Boy Scouts growing up," he admitted.

"Oh, trust me, I *wanted* to be. But . . . you know, that whole thing where they're homophobic and transphobic as fuck. Anyway, it did teach me an important lesson."

"What's that?"

Ginsberg sighed at his casted arm. "That you don't always get what you want."

Derrick put down the sheet he was holding and took Ginsberg's face in both hands. "Yeah, well, here's another lesson."

"Yeah?" Ginsberg breathed, eyes slipping closed as Derrick drew closer. "What's that?"

"That sometimes you do."

Despite five of the eight guest rooms being occupied—well, four not counting Ginsberg's but either way that was insane for a Thursday—the place felt empty without Ginsberg.

And simultaneously far too busy, considering he had no one to help him set the tables or cook breakfast for the guests or walk Victoria or make up the rooms or do the laundry or chop firewood or clean the common areas or set out afternoon tea or wash the endless dishes or greet new guests or talk to current ones or turn down beds while Ginsberg was gone all day. He might've been just a little bit grumpy checking in a new couple here for a weekend *Wolf's Landing* set-tour-slash-pilgrimage. And perhaps could've given a little more time and effort to dinner recommendations for the newlyweds. And probably could've bitched less to himself while scrubbing out the ridiculous heart-shaped *en suite* tub that the guests put bubble bath or some shit in despite clear instructions not to and that had left a horrible residue behind.

It was awfully nice not having to stress anymore about paying his bills—heck, he'd even been able to hire an electrician and a plumber to fix the third-floor wiring and water-heating problems—but Jesus, who knew running a B&B was so much *work*? And clearly he hadn't been appreciating Ginsberg's contribution enough because it all seemed like so much more of a burden without him.

Better get used to it, bud. This is how it's gonna be all the time once that cast comes off.

Working all day, then alone all night. No way would Ginsberg be staying here once he had the money to get his own place. It was too far from the studio, too out in the country, too distant from the culture a guy like Ginsberg needed.

Plus, at the rate things were going, Derrick was going to need Ginsberg's room soon.

Maybe they'd try at dating while living separately, but eventually Ginsberg would remember that his life was way too exciting to want a boring asshole like Derrick hanging around.

And even if he didn't, *Wolf's Landing* would end one day, or his stunt work on it would slow down enough for him to need another job, or they'd replace him, and then he'd be off to somewhere else. Not like he'd ever find another stunt job here in Bluewater Bay; it wasn't exactly Hollywood or even Vancouver. Nothing shot here but one silly show. And when that left, not only would the work leave, but so would every drop of bustle and commerce; they'd be back to two restaurants, zero souvenir shops, a used bookstore, and a second-run movie theater if they were lucky. And a bunch of bars that catered to loggers, of course.

Not a single one of which would make Ginsberg happy. Which meant that no matter how happy Ginsberg made Derrick—and vice versa—Derrick really had been fooling himself this past month. Living a stupid, harmful, dangerous lie: that they could be good together, that they could have something together, *make* something together.

But maybe . . . Maybe they should talk about this. That seemed like the sort of thing Ginsberg would want, right? For Derrick not to make decisions on his own that would affect them both. For Derrick to *respect* him.

And yeah, he did. And he owed Ginsberg that much, at least. Even if Ginsberg, ever the optimist, would probably be unable to see the situation for what it really was. In which case, it'd be up to Derrick to protect them both, wouldn't it?

And that was why, when Ginsberg stumbled home around eleven, tired and tipsy and in far too good a mood to ruin, Derrick let the kid take him to bed and didn't say a word about his worries. Just let Ginsberg giggle and gush over how great it felt to be back on set and how awesome it was to see everyone again and what an amazing time they'd had at that ridiculous hipster bar (Derrick's words, not Ginsberg's) after wrap and how excited he was to be going in tomorrow even though he had to sit back and watch the replacement stunt double do all the cool things.

When Derrick couldn't bear to listen to Ginsberg drifting away from him anymore, he kissed him quiet and fucked him into the mattress and passed out holding on a little too tight, then let Ginsberg sleep while he dragged his ass out of bed at 5 a.m. to get ready for the early-bird breakfast.

Ginsberg popped into the kitchen around 8:30, gave Derrick a lingering, fervent kiss that tasted of toothpaste, and headed straight for the espresso machine. "Breakfast?" Derrick asked, and it was strange how important the answer to that question was, how badly he wanted—needed—Ginsberg to stay, even just for a little while.

But then he noticed that Ginsberg was pouring his coffee into a travel mug.

"Can't. Smells delish, but I'll be late if I stay. I'll eat at the craft table." He flashed Derrick a playful grin. "They have *smoothies*."

"We could make smoothies," Derrick groused, and realized how petulant he sounded only when Ginsberg's lips pressed tight to hold back a laugh.

"Indeed we could," Ginsberg said, but he still just pecked Derrick on the lips and turned to leave the kitchen. "We've got night stunts on the schedule, so I expect to be very late. Don't wait up, 'kay?"

Great. Just great. But he pasted on a grin and made himself wave and said, "Sure thing. Have fun!"

"Will do—you too!" Ginsberg called over his shoulder as he walked through the crowded little dining room and out the front door.

Forget fun. The day was *long*. And grueling, even for Ginsberg, who was only coaching the double rather than actually doing the stunts. God, night-shoots sucked. Especially when you had long day-shoots leading up to them because you were on day six of an eight-day shoot and already like twelve days behind schedule. The overtime pay was awesome, but trudging home at 3 a.m.? Significantly less awesome.

He didn't dare risk waking Derrick—the poor guy had to get up in two hours anyway to deal with the early-bird crowd—so he just tiptoed up to his own room, set his alarm, and fell into bed. After the past few weeks spent with Cuddly McCuddlerson, he wasn't quite sure what to do with all the space and freedom he had, and as tired as he was, sleep didn't come easy.

And didn't shake easy, either, when the alarm buzzed at noon. He dragged his clothes into the bathroom down the hall, which was empty even though the floor was nearly full (Fridays downright *buzzed* here now)—one advantage, he supposed, to rolling out of bed so late. Derrick would be somewhere in the rooms now, changing sheets, making beds, and cleaning bathrooms. Probably best not to bother him, considering how much work he had to do on his own without Ginsberg around to help. So Ginsberg slipped down to the kitchen, waving to the guests he passed on the way, and helped himself to some coffee and leftover pastries. He helped himself to one other thing too—something he needed for a little surprise he was planning for his man. Then he wrote a quick note—"Had to run, back very late. Off Monday tho. Miss you!"—and headed for the studio.

And into a complete and utter gong show. The guest stunt performer they were supposed to throw out a three-story window at 4 p.m. decided to start projectile vomiting instead, which meant that not only did *that* scene get canceled, but so did all his other scenes. Which meant basically rearranging what remained of the day—which rearranged every stunt on the schedule, which rearranged Ginsberg's whole reason for being there. It also meant that he'd have to come in Monday, but hey, at least he and Derrick would have the weekend together.

He talked to Natalya about sticking around to rehearse with his replacement, but she rightly pointed out that staying late tonight and also coming in Monday would violate the union's 56-hour weekend rule, and sent him home in time for dinner.

He had two stops to make before he could head back to the B&B, though. Because the more he'd been thinking about Derrick over there by himself, doing all that hard work, the more guilty he'd been feeling. Sure, the B&B wasn't his responsibility, but he and Derrick were in a relationship now, and being a good boyfriend meant making your partner's problems *your* problems too. And frankly, he was *proud* of Derrick. Maybe he hadn't yet figured out how to tell the guy he loved him, but he could certainly *show* him, right? With a surprise that'd be special, personal, important to them both. Something deep and sincere but also a little funny. And, let's face it, something he could afford.

And he'd planned just the thing.

CHAPTER SEVENTEEN

What the hell was he gonna tell Ginsberg?

Other than to book reservations or chip away at overdue e-bills, Derrick hadn't been checking his email much lately.

There hadn't *ever* been a time when he'd consistently checked his email, but he was even worse now that he had a million other urgent responsibilities. Which was why it was such a shocker that he'd somehow managed to spot an email from Steve—one of his old logging-camp buddies—in between the emails about room amenities and advertisements for dick pills.

Subject line: WANT SUM WORK???

He almost hadn't clicked it. *Already got plenty of work right here where I belong, thanks. Work that's important even if nobody sees it.*

And then he'd sat back in his seat and thought about how Ginsberg—the guy who'd gotten him thinking that way in the first place—hadn't been around in days. It seemed that making beds and pouring coffee was good enough for Derrick, but not good enough for *him*.

And could Derrick blame him? The guy was a stunt actor on a hit TV show. He rubbed elbows with celebrities and had a staff of people making him smoothies and bringing him bottles of imported water. Could any shitty B&B—even one experiencing an uptick in revenue—compare to that life?

Of course not. But it didn't make Derrick feel any better about being stuck here while Ginsberg was elsewhere. About the fact that Ginsberg championed the B&B out of one side of his mouth, but then went running off to his infinitely cooler and more fulfilling life, leaving Derrick to the day-to-day unglamorous grind.

Not that the camp job was all that great by Hollywood standards, either, but at least he wouldn't be expected to wait on other people hand and foot. At least he'd have someone cooking his meals too—even if it wasn't craft services making cheese platters and sparkling fruit juice or whatever the hell celebrities ate and drank.

At least he wouldn't be here, feeling like an asshole, waiting around like some housewife for Ginsberg to come home to him—and knowing that sooner or later he just . . . wouldn't.

That was the worst part. Ginsberg had gotten him to see the validity and the meaning of this place, of this life, had helped him to accept it and embrace it, and now that he was good and tied down, Ginsberg was walking away.

And what if this life wasn't meaningful without Ginsberg? What if it wasn't enough? Two months ago, Derrick could have walked away from all this, but now that the place was becoming a success, it wasn't so easy. Ginsberg had tied him to this, and he wasn't even sure if it was something he wanted, or just something he wanted because Ginsberg wanted it *for* him. Without Ginsberg, would this all fall apart?

And if it did, where would that leave Derrick?

Miserable. Trapped. Forced to do a job that wasn't right for him, that he didn't feel good about, because he couldn't say no to the money.

He should have sent Ginsberg away when he had the chance. *Actually* sent him away, that was. As in *kicked him out* like he'd planned to before Ginsberg had revealed he was trans and Derrick had gotten all softhearted and cowardly. Not played stupid games, not tried to manipulate him into deciding to leave on his own, not attempted a bunch of halfhearted schemes.

Now it was too late.

He scrubbed his hands over his face and stared at his computer screen.

WANT SUM WORK???

Or maybe it wasn't.

Two hours later, Derrick was folding sheets and thinking about ordering a pizza—he actually had some spending cash now, didn't have to eat beans from a can anymore—wondering how he was going to broach the topic of shuttering this place with Ginsberg, when the bell over the front door rang.

He ignored it. Couldn't get in without a key, and only guests (and Jim) had those. Probably just someone heading out to dinner or coming in with their day's shopping, and his obligations to his guests were done for the day. If someone really needed him, they'd knock on his door.

Nobody did, though. There was just some rattling around from the dining room—probably a guest helping themselves to some coffee or fruit or the leftover snacks from afternoon tea. Best leave them to it; he had more important things to do now anyway, like (laundry) imagining how Ginsberg's happy, glowy face would shut right down when he told the kid he didn't want to do this anymore. Or . . . maybe Ginsberg would be relieved. He had a doc's appointment next week to get the cast off, and it sure would be easier for Ginsberg to go running back to his exciting Hollywood life if he wasn't dragging some old small-town lumberjack behind him. It wasn't too late to cut ties. It's not like they were in love or any of that mushy crap, right?

But they were definitely *something*.

"Honey, I'm home!"

Something. Definitely.

Derrick cringed. What the hell was Ginsberg doing back so early? Derrick should have had at least six more hours to agonize over what to say.

Instead he greeted Ginsberg with as enthusiastic a "Hey" as he could manage when the kid let himself in, a huge grin plastered on his face and a cloth shopping bag dangling from his casted wrist. Derrick unfolded the sheet he'd just finished folding and held it up in front of his face to give himself just a few more seconds of privacy.

Ginsberg hooked the edge of the sheet with his good hand, drawing it aside like a curtain so he could press a kiss to Derrick's mouth—a kiss that landed on Derrick's jaw thanks to a last-second dodge.

Ginsberg's brow furrowed, but he shook it off almost instantly and purred, "Surprise," his voice unfairly sexy. "Home early. Want some help with the laundry?"

"You know you can't fold for shit with your bum hand." Derrick resented that he'd even bothered to offer when he couldn't follow through. Ha. Just like a . . . what'd they call those things? A microcosm. Yeah. Like a microcosm of this whole fucked-up situation, Ginsberg coming in and offering to help make this place thrive when he knew damn well he couldn't follow through on *that*, either.

Ginsberg pulled away. Seemed to take in Derrick's expression for the first time. That furrowed brow returned, this time with pursed lips to match. Derrick could practically see the potential questions cycling through Ginsberg's mind in the too-long silence that followed, but eventually the kid plastered his smile back on—not quite as big or as easy as before, though—and said, "I have bad news and good news. Which do you want first?"

No real question what a crusty old asshole like Derrick would pick: "Gimme the bad."

Let's see if it's worse than the bad news I have for you.

"So the stunt actor guesting this week got hella sick today, I mean, like, puke *everywhere*"—he made an irritatingly adorable little exploding sound with pursed lips and poofed cheeks and jazz hands—"so we had to rearrange the whole shooting schedule. Which on the one hand meant I got to come home early, *ta-da*! but on the other hand means I have to go back Monday to help shoot the missed scenes. And I know, I *know* I promised I'd stay and help out on Monday and that we'd run errands together and all that jazz, but it's just one more day, okay?"

"Yeah. Sure." Derrick stared at the wall to his left, the one with the inexplicably framed *Welcome to Trenton!* postcard. One day, every day, what did it matter?

"But there's good news, too!" Ginsberg blurted. "I'll be in all weekend, and I thought we could try some new recipes, hit up the grocery store, really step up the breakfast game, you know?" When Derrick said nothing, Ginsberg scrunched his mouth, shifted his weight from one foot to the other, and then unhooked the cloth bag from around his bum arm. Derrick didn't mean to make him so uncomfortable, but it wasn't like he was feeling all that great himself. "So I, uh, I got you a present. I mean, *us* a present, I suppose, but I hope you'll like it and I spent like an hour picking it out so, um—" He thrust the bag into Derrick's lap, inexplicably blushing. "Here."

There was nothing Derrick wanted less than to accept a gift from Ginsberg. Not now. Not like this. He had half a mind to shove it right back into the kid's arms.

Except for that part where right from the beginning, right from that first halfhearted prank to try to drive Ginsberg out, Derrick had been a fucking coward.

Still was.

"I don't think—" he tried.

"Open it! C'mon man. You're killing me. Just open it. It's not an engagement ring, all right?" He let out a very forced laugh. "Or a bomb. Not sure which you'd think was worse."

Well that was just fucking uncalled for. And did the kid have to look *quite* so much like a kicked puppy?

Apparently so.

Fine. Okay. He opened the damn bag.

And came face-to-face with something . . . pink?

Was this a fucking joke?

He dared a sharp glance at Ginsberg, who was staring at him with this weird hopeful look, chewing his lip and twisting the hem of his T-shirt in his hand.

Derrick pulled the pink thing out of the bag. Pink with white polka dots, to be specific. And frills.

"That one's mine," Ginsberg said, then clamped his mouth shut.

Derrick set it aside, not even bothering to unfold it to see what shape the pink frilly fabric took.

There was another pink ball at the bottom of the bag. This one was . . . printed with some kind of pattern? Derrick pulled it out of the bag as if it were a bomb—or an engagement ring, sure, fine, whatever—and unfolded it over his lap.

The pattern was of donuts. Donuts with pink icing and yellow sprinkles. Bright girly donuts. Printed on a frilly, pink, dress-shaped . . . apron.

"I had to buy yours in plus-size. I didn't think the standard one would tie." Still trying to joke, but his voice was visibly strained now.

Derrick clutched at the fabric. His hands were shaking.

"The fuck is this?"

"Aprons for us! You know, I thought if we were gonna be spending all this time cooking together we needed some—"

"Just shut up," Derrick snapped. He balled the apron and stuffed it back into the bag—barely refrained from hurling it across the room, or in the trash. "Just . . . just stop talking. Stop talking like you're gonna be cooking with me. Stop talking like you belong here. You don't. You never did."

"The hell?" Ginsberg choked out.

Derrick couldn't look at him. "You're fucking making fun of me!" *Just like all the kids at school all my life.* "You got me neutered, doing laundry, baking cupcakes, now you put me in a fucking apron like a housewife. You think this is some kind of joke? You think *I'm* some kind of joke?"

"What? No!" Derrick felt the couch dip as Ginsberg sat down beside him. Not touching, though. Derrick very deliberately kept his eyes on his fisted hands. He was *not* going to be placated here. "I . . . I thought you were over this macho crap. I also got myself an apron if you didn't notice. If I'm making fun of you, then I'm making fun of myself too."

Ginsberg touched a hand to Derrick's shoulder, waited a beat. Derrick shrugged him off. Another beat, tense silence, a near-theatric sigh, and then Ginsberg stood from the couch. Derrick was still too mad to look at the kid, but he imagined Ginsberg's arms folded across his chest, awkward with the cast.

When he spoke again, his usually playful, optimistic voice was tense. "And in case it didn't occur to you, it's a lot more compromising for *me* to wear a girly apron than it is for you. Nobody's calling *your* manhood into question . . . not that you'd know it by how fucking defensive you're always acting about it!"

"Oh fucking save me the lecture! You're not my shrink." Derrick found himself on his feet now too, staring the kid down at last. Ginsberg looked as wounded and furious as he was. His heart was pounding so hard he could feel it in his hands, in his temples, in his gut. "And while we're at it, you're not my life coach either. You're not my business partner. You're not my boyfriend. You're a piece of ass.

You're some city-boy meddler, and I should have kicked you out when I had the chance!"

". . . Kicked me out?"

"Yeah, kicked you out. What did you fucking think, my clothes dryer was actually broken? That I didn't know how to make a pot of damn coffee? That I put you in the darkest, draftiest, lumpiest third-floor walk-up by accident?"

Ginsberg's face was pale. Like he was about to faint. Or like he was about to sock Derrick right in the nose.

But he just stood there. "You . . ."

"Yeah. I never wanted you here. I never wanted your help. I wanted to shut this place down and forget all about the fucking nightmare that made it mine and go back to doing some real work. *Men's* work. Not . . ." He kicked the bag at his feet, toppling it. "Not *pink cupcake apron* work."

"And yet you still *fucked* me? Even though you wanted me gone this entire time?" Ginsberg asked. His voice was soft now.

Derrick's anger went out like a candle on a gusty day. He hadn't . . . it wasn't like he'd *molested* the kid or something. "I didn't— It wasn't like that."

"Then what was it like, huh? How come you didn't just—*ha!*— man up and ask me to go? Why the procrastination? You— I— Oh God." Ginsberg blinked, swallowed, blinked again. His eyes were shining, damn everything all to hell. "You knew you wanted me gone sooner rather than later, but once you found out about me being trans you had to . . . what, wait for a chance to examine my junk? See for yourself how it feels to fuck a trans guy? Because no matter the circumstances, you people *always* make it about sex with us and you . . . you . . . what, *seduced* me? Bided your time, decided you could throw me out on the street the minute you got your fetishistic fill of me?"

"No!" Derrick protested. He hadn't even *thought* about that. Sure he'd wanted to have sex with Ginsberg, wondered what it would feel like, but not because he had a fetish! Ginsberg being trans had nothing to do with Derrick's attraction. He hadn't cared about Ginsberg's "junk" one bit, up until he was getting cozy with it. "Wait, what do you mean, 'you people'? You think this is because I'm . . . I'm . . . normal and you're—?"

Ginsberg's eyes widened. Derrick could see the full roundness of his irises and they were *black*. "I *am* fucking normal, Derrick. It's you with your pervy freak-show sate-your-curiosity-and-then-toss-people bullshit that's fucking sick and twisted here."

"How many times do I have to tell you it was *not like that*? I couldn't kick you out right away because once you said you were . . . you know, I was worried you'd think I was kicking you out *because* of it! That you'd sue me! So I just tried to . . . convince you to leave on your own. But the longer you stuck around . . ." *The more I started to love you.* But he couldn't say that. Not now. "Okay yeah, we wound up fucking, but it's not like I planned on it, okay? I just couldn't close this place down with you here!"

Ginsberg jabbed a finger in his face. "One, you're a fucking coward. Two, I think that's actually fucking worse. Three—" he turned his finger on the door. "Get the fuck out."

"You can't kick me out. I *live* here."

Ginsberg startled at that, but then he nodded. Nodded to himself, closed his eyes, seemed to count to three, then opened them again. "Okay, okay. So I can't kick you out. I can still do *this*."

He reared back and punched Derrick right between the eyes.

CHAPTER EIGHTEEN

He woke up to someone kissing his ear. Tonguing his ear, actually. He smiled and chuckled. "Gins' stopit," he muttered, swatting playfully.

"Oh you are capital P Pathetic."

Derrick's eyes shot open. That was not Ginsberg's voice.

That was *Jim.*

A distinctly pissed-off Jim, looming over him with his arms crossed.

Derrick was sprawled on his back on the floor.

Victoria was tonguing his ear.

"Gah!" he shouted, and sat up. His face throbbed.

Shit. Ginsberg had punched him in the face.

For a little guy, he had a hell of a sucker punch.

"What are you doing here?" he asked Jim, who was clearly making a point of not giving him a hand up. "Looking for some rebound action?"

"Oh shut it, you pig Neanderthal. Like I'd ever stoop *that* low again. Be grateful I didn't leave you two years earlier, when I finally figured out that great sex didn't justify putting up with an asshole. I almost did, you know, but then your parents died and I . . ."

Jim's lips pressed into a thin white line, and Derrick almost didn't notice the pain of that spat-out truth over the shock of seeing Jim angry and indignant enough to lob it. He'd never been this mad before. Not even during their worst blow-up fights. Not even that one time Derrick had slapped him on the ass and told him to make him a sandwich. Not even when they broke up.

Well, he was sure pissed off now. And Derrick knew exactly why.

"Ginsberg . . ." he groaned, gingerly touching the bridge of his nose.

"Is the one who sent me. Wanted to make sure his punch didn't knock you straight to dead. Now that I see you're alive though, I gotta say it's taking all my willpower not to stomp your head. Wouldn't want to ruin your mom's fab floral area rug."

"Looking out for me even from the grave," Derrick quipped mirthlessly.

"I said *shut it*. If your mother really was watching from the grave, I guarantee she'd be fighting the urge to stomp your head, too. Seriously, didn't you learn your lesson treating *me* like I was disposable? Or did the fact that I was stupid enough to stick around and be your friend somehow make you think it was okay to do that to the people you love? What the hell is *wrong* with you?"

"The hell is wrong with *me*? The hell is wrong with *you*?"

"Besides convincing myself all these years that despite your macho bullshit you're still a good guy deep down? Nothing." He flipped Derrick a double bird and said, "How many fingers am I holding up?"

"Aw, c'mon, don't be like that." Derrick rubbed at his temples, squeezed his eyes closed. When he opened them again, Jim was still waving his two middle fingers. "Fine," he said. "Two, okay?"

"Ginsberg was the best thing to ever happen to you, Derrick. And I'm including myself in the rankings there." He finally dropped his hands, but then raised one again to point in Derrick's face. "You want to throw that away, I am *not* sticking around to watch it happen. You're obviously not dying, so you just sit here in your own mess alone. I'm gone."

"Jim, wait!" Derrick struggled to his feet as Jim stormed out of the living room, no idea of why this was so important to him—he and Jim had never exactly been *good*, had they?—but desperate to fix it anyway. He ran into the kitchen, then the dining room, watching Jim stomp down the hall. "Jim!"

Jim turned, hand on the front doorknob, and Derrick dared to hope he was coming back, but he just snarled, "Oh and by the way. You owe me eight hundred bucks for all that baking I did. Figure out your own damn breakfast tomorrow."

He slammed the door behind him.

Shit.

Derrick headed back to his room, trying hard to ignore the fact that any guests inside the house had surely heard every word of his arguments with Ginsberg *and* Jim. At least nobody was in the downstairs hallway or the common rooms he passed. *No, probably gleefully lurking behind a corner upstairs, drinking in every drop of drama.*

Derrick plopped on the couch, head in his hands. Changed his mind and went to find some fucking aspirin. He passed his computer on the way to the medicine cabinet, and was drawn right to it on the way back. Opened up his email.

WANT SUM WORK???

There was real clarity, he realized, in the wake of so much anger. Ginsberg was gone, probably forever. Jim was gone too, also probably forever. And his parents were gone, definitely forever. So what the hell was tying him to this place anymore anyway? This had all been such a colossally bad idea, right from the start. He'd just been thinking too much with the wrong head to see the truth.

He clicked Reply. *Yeah, I'm in. When and where, and for how long?*

Next step was to email all the booked guests and cancel their reservations, but that could wait until his head didn't hurt quite so much. Maybe a cup of coffee would help. He didn't feel like messing with that ridiculous fucking espresso machine, but there was reasonably fresh coffee in the beverage dispenser in the dining room, and if it was good enough for his precious *guests*, then it was good enough for him. He didn't need all that froo-frah fancy drink shit anyway.

He stomped out into the dining room, just fucking *daring* any of the motherfuckers staying under his roof to get in his way now. Snatched one of the many mismatched mugs he and Ginsberg had thrifted one day and stormed up to the breakfast bar.

Stopped short.

Because the landscape watercolor of the beached rowboat that used to hang in that very spot was gone, replaced by a shiny new shadow-box frame. And inside it, his mother's floral apron, lovingly displayed.

There was a card wedged into the frame. Derrick had half a mind to leave it, but he couldn't stop himself. He plucked it from its place and ripped open the foil-lined envelope.

The card inside was one of those fancy handmade things you could buy in the trinket shops on Main Street, handstamped on recycled paper. Derrick didn't really care about any of that, not compared to what was written inside.

Here's to honoring your past and embracing our future.
I love you.
Ginsberg

The card fluttered out of Derrick's nerveless fingers and onto the breakfast bar.

I love you.

Our future.

Ours.

He picked it up again. The writing on the card blurred.

Macho or no, it didn't fucking stop him from dropping to his knees to cry. He gave in to it for a minute or two—had no choice, really—but the longer he knelt there like some little kid, the more he realized he had no idea what he was crying *for*. Ginsberg didn't love him. He loved an *idea* of him, the man Ginsberg had spent all this time trying to shape him into. And seriously, fuck that anyway. Wasn't that why he'd kicked him out? Why this could never, ever have worked?

So then why did it feel like someone was cleaving an ax through his chest?

Because he loved Ginsberg, too. Or maybe just the idea of Ginsberg, in turn.

And that was why this was for the best.

Strange ceiling.

Ginsberg stared up at the new light fixture and gave himself a moment to remember. He always did eventually.

Jim. I'm at Jim's place.

Because Derrick had kicked him out. Because he'd *walked* out. Stormed out, even. Because Derrick wasn't the man Ginsberg had believed him to be after all.

Jim, on the other hand, had been twice the man.

Just a shame he didn't have a guest bedroom.

As thankful as he was for the place to stay, Ginsberg would be lying if he said he wasn't disappointed to be back on somebody's couch again.

And to think, just yesterday he'd finally convinced himself he'd found a home. A real, forever home and a man to share it with besides.

Oh well. At least Derrick's outburst had ended things between them quickly, rather than dragging them out for months on end as resentment grew and turned into hostility, like it had with his parents all those years ago. Better to get it over with.

Easier said than done, though. He scrubbed at stinging eyes with his good hand, uselessly trying to talk himself out of the grief and the sharp stab of betrayal.

He'd thought Derrick was different. He really had.

But he wasn't, and Ginsberg would have to accept that.

It might help that his cast was coming off soon and he could throw himself back into his work. Find some new housing so he wasn't overstaying his welcome on Jim's couch—something he could afford with the housing stipend he'd started collecting again when he'd gone back to work on set. Seventy-five bucks a day wasn't much, not in a town whose entire population was only ten times the size of a cast and crew who all needed places to crash, and especially not with so many tourists flocking in. But he'd make it work. He always had. He'd get his life back and treat this whole thing with Derrick like the passing phase it clearly was.

But God, it fucking hurt. It *hurt*.

He'd forgotten how much it could hurt.

Good thing he didn't have to work today; he'd just have spent the whole shift crying on Carter's shoulder while the poor guy was trying to accomplish things.

He wandered into the kitchen instead—didn't bother to shower or even change out of the clothes he'd slept in—and found Jim humming over the stove. In a pink apron, *of course*, because the universe hadn't kicked him in his nonexistent nuts enough this week.

Jim turned around, a cup of coffee in one hand and a frosted cupcake in the other. "Morning, sweetie," he said, offering Ginsberg his breakfast of champions. He sounded as subdued and miserable as Ginsberg felt, smiling wanly when Ginsberg took a sip of the coffee and a big lick of the frosting off the cupcake. "I baked. I do that when life hands me lemons, because fuck lemonade."

He stepped aside and swept his arm at the counter behind him, which was littered with cupcakes and cookies and the pastries Jim normally delivered to the B&B every morning.

"You didn't have to go to all this trouble for me," Ginsberg said.

"Don't even. Sweets may not solve your problems, but they *will* boost your endorphins. Or something. Just stuff your face for me, please?"

Jim was right. And maybe Ginsberg shouldn't be eating like this when he wasn't keeping up his exercise routine, but you know what? Fuck that too. He stuffed half a cupcake in his mouth and smiled at Jim around it. "Fank oo," he managed, still chewing. It *was* good.

So why was he starting to cry again?

"Oh, *honey*," Jim cooed, and stepped forward to wrap Ginsberg in a big, tight hug. Some coffee sloshed onto the floor, but Jim didn't seem to care. "You just go right ahead and cry it out. Unlike *some* people, I think expressing your emotions is good for you and doesn't make you any less of a man."

The jibe at Derrick just made him even sadder, which kind of made him angry because why should he be crying over such a colossal ass? Which . . . helped. Anger hurt less.

But he cried anyway. Let Jim hold him because maybe this wasn't home, but Jim was his friend and he needed one right now.

Jim was *such* a good friend, in fact, that they spent the entire weekend sitting at the kitchen table or curled up on the couch, subsisting on baked goods and '90s chick flicks and occasional crying jags. By the time he had to go back to work on Monday, he was feeling . . . well, if not better, then at least *stable*. And probably five pounds heavier too, but he'd fix that as soon as the damn cast came off, and anyway, he was pretty sure it'd been worth it because he knew there was someone in the world who cared for him and accepted him, even if it was his ex's ex.

Still, he could only impose on Jim for so long; if his early adult years had taught him anything, it was how easy it was to outstay your welcome. So back at the studio, crying again except this time in Carter's trailer (even though he'd *sworn* to himself he wasn't going to anymore, that he was all cried out), he took the invitation Carter offered to stay at his and Levi's place instead. That big old rattling mansion on the outskirts of town, where Levi had spent so long hiding from the world until *Wolf's Landing*—and then Carter—had come into his life. Seemed fitting for Ginsberg to hide out there awhile himself. It wouldn't be home, but it'd be stable for a bit. And it'd let him pocket his stipend, put it toward all those medical bills looming over his head.

The day started looking up even more when Natalya told him he'd be going from daily to weekly, starting now. Since he probably wouldn't be able to perform any stunts for six or eight weeks, and Natalya didn't *really* seem to need his help coordinating, and even his replacement was getting into the swing of moving like Carter, Ginsberg had the sneaking suspicion that Carter and Levi had intervened on his behalf. Seen how miserable he was and pressured Anna and Finn into finding *something* for him to do so he wouldn't sit in that mansion all day and wallow.

Derrick probably would've been furious about that kind of interference, his poor fragile manly-man ego unable to accept help. But Ginsberg was glad of it. Grateful. Being on set, surrounded by the cast and crew he'd grown to know and love these past three and a half years, feeling useful even if he wasn't really . . . it all helped to ease the sting. Helped him to remember how great his life had been before he'd met that effemiphobic asshole. How great it could be *again*, damn it.

Eventually.

CHAPTER NINETEEN

"You sure you wanna stay at camp on your week off?" Randall asked. He was stuffing dirty clothes and pilfered water bottles into his rucksack. "I can't fucking wait to get back to civilization. Gonna get some Starbucks."

The guy was as rugged as they came, even among the loggers—late forties and rock solid with a full beard and arms covered in cheesy tattoos—but he drank more frappuccinos than a teenage girl.

Derrick shook his head. "Nah, man. Nothing for me there. I think spending some time in the woods will be good for me, you know?"

"You've just spent an entire month in the woods." Derrick shrugged. "Man, usually when guys say that, they're trying to avoid their old lady."

Derrick scoffed. Not even close, but he wasn't about to come out to the guy. About being gay *or* about being all torn up about the city boy he'd left behind.

"What you gonna do here all week anyway? You know they won't let you work. Not now that some pencil pusher workers' comp asshole in Seattle's going over everybody's hours. And you still gotta pay the camp fees if you don't go."

"I can swing the twenty-five bucks a day. And camp's packed to the gills; I'm sure I'll find someone to entertain me."

"You not even gonna go home for Thanksgiving?"

What for? His parents were gone. Ginsberg was gone. Even Jim hated him. "Nah. I like it here."

For just a second, Randall looked like he might say something serious, or at least reassuring, but then he clapped Derrick on the shoulder and said, "Just keep your dick out of the camp cooks. Or at least wrap it."

Derrick pulled a face. "Thanks for that, but really not necessary."

"Well if you're gonna be in here jerking it the whole time, don't leave your cumsocks around for me to find."

"Go the fuck home, Randall."

"See ya after turkey day." The door shut behind him, and Derrick was alone.

Just him and the woods. No internet or cell phone, no fancy coffees or pink donuts or sheets to be folded. No floral anything, no watercolor paintings, no frilly aprons.

No sweet, sexy, relentlessly upbeat Ginsberg.

Just scratchy sheets and a hard twin bed and thinner-than-paper camp trailer walls. Meat three meals a day and nobody'd even heard of quinoa.

So why the hell wasn't he relieved?

Worse, why was he so fucking *upset*?

He didn't have long to mope about it, though, because before long there was another knock on his door.

"C'min," he called, shocked by how shaky his voice came out. *Get it the fuck together before somebody sees you like this.*

The door opened. One of the younger guys poked his head in. "Oh, you *are* still here! Cool, man. Listen, some of us guys are gonna take over the camp TV and watch the *Wolf's Landing* midseason finale tonight. There's a marathon on before, starting at . . ." He checked his watch. "In about fifteen minutes, actually, if you need to get caught up. You in? I know you said you never got around to watching it, but I figure you're from Bluewater Bay, maybe you finally wanna see what all the fuss is about."

"Well I don't," Derrick snarled. "But fuck it. Better than sitting in here. You got beer?"

"Yeah. C'mon. Cook even made pizza. We all gotta be there or else Andrew's gonna try and put it on fucking *Storage Wars* again. Strength in numbers, man." He held out his hand for a fist bump, and for some inexplicable reason it reminded Derrick so damn much of Ginsberg he wanted to break down and cry.

Again.

Which made the thin camp walls all the more horrifying.

He'd gladly put up with a hundred nights of listening to the guy in the room next to him jerking off or the guy on the other side blasting bad rap music if it meant neither of them heard his late night self-pity sessions. And as for *Wolf's Landing*, well, he'd watch it just to prove to himself that he fucking *could*, because men didn't back down or hide from their problems, and they sure as fuck didn't pine and weep over their ex on TV. If Derrick even spotted Ginsberg. After all, the whole point of the guy's job was to go unnoticed.

The rec room was packed to the rafters by the time they got there, every couch and a slew of folding chairs already occupied. Looked like half the guys in camp, though no way half the camp had the day off at the same time. Must've been more people here than he'd realized these past few weeks. He tried not to think about how much of this lumber would probably end up right back in Bluewater Bay, going in to all the new hotels and restaurants and houses the developers couldn't build fast enough. Ruining his sleepy little town. Another year, there'd be more Hollywood than Washington there.

God, fuck *Wolf's Landing* anyway.

And yet obviously it had *something* going for it, to cram thirty guys at a logging camp into a room to watch the damn thing for the next eight hours.

Derrick grabbed a folding chair and made himself a space near the beer. He had no idea what the show was about beyond "werewolves," and the marathon was replaying the first half of season 4, but they started with a long "Previously On" that sort of made sense. Three episodes, four beers, and two slices of pizza later, he reluctantly admitted to himself that the show was good. Like, *really* good. He tried very hard not to spend more time looking for Ginsberg than following all the intertwining story threads, but the more he drank, the harder and harder that got. He'd figured out just by body type that Ginsberg had to be the double for the guy who played Gabriel Hanford, since he'd said he was doubling for one of the leads, and there were only two, and he looked nothing at all like the big, bulky action-star type playing Rolling Thunder.

Truth was, he didn't look all that much like the Gabriel actor, either. What was his name . . . Carter something? He'd met him that night at the coffee shop, but he hadn't been paying as much attention as he probably should've been. Carter and Ginsberg didn't match at all in the face, really, and even the body wasn't *quite* right. Derrick strongly suspected he was the only one who'd noticed that, though, given how carefully Ginsberg blended himself in, holding himself and moving exactly like Carter. Fact was, Ginsberg must've been hired for how *talented* he was, rather than for being a carbon copy of this Carter guy.

And boy did the Gabriel character do a lot of stunts. Fights and throws and car crashes and jumps through windows and more fights and once even being on fire.

And, ah, there Ginsberg was again, crashing through a china cabinet in the middle of a fistfight, glass everywhere.

The whole room gasped as one, like a bunch of pearl-clutching soccer moms.

Derrick grabbed another beer.

Fuck, he missed Ginsberg. He was man enough to admit that to himself now, four beers down. Even man enough to admit that he missed the comforts of the B&B—his own room, the cozy fireplace, the soaking tub in his en suite, even that stupid espresso machine in the kitchen and those fancy little pastries at breakfast and teatime. He hated freezing his balls off out here every day, the blisters on his hands, the soreness in his muscles and feet, the utter lack of privacy, the sad shower heads, the smell of sawdust and the stickiness of sap all over everything.

He hadn't spoken to Ginsberg in a month, and he was pretty sure he hadn't *smiled* in a month either. Frankly, he was starting to wonder if maybe he'd made some kind of colossal fucking mistake.

"Oh hey, hey, check this out!" Someone slapped him on the shoulder, and his beer sloshed onto his jeans. He turned to give the guy the stinkeye, but the guy seemed so fucking excited he didn't even notice. "Coming up, look, look. This car crash? This is so *badass*, man. Shit went wrong and the stunt double broke his wrist in three places, and they used the *actual footage* of that happening."

Oh no. Oh no no no. The beer and pizza went sour in Derrick's gut. He didn't want to see this. They were talking about Ginsberg *getting hurt* and he *didn't want to see this.*

"Look look look! This is so cool, man. Riiiiiiight . . . there!"

He looked.

"Jesus, watch that guy fly!"

Ginsberg had rolled up the hood, smashed into the windshield, and launched over the roof of the car, landing in a writhing heap in the street ten or fifteen feet away.

God. Derrick felt sick. What sort of person *did* that to themselves for a living anyway?

A hugely fucking brave one, that's who.

"Actually," someone piped up from the couch, "I heard he *wasn't* always a guy."

Derrick barely heard the chorus of *What?* and *No way!* over the sudden rushing of blood in his ears.

"Yeah, saw an interview in some supermarket rag, I dunno. Said he was born a chick."

"Huh. Wonder what the plumbing's like down there. Some kinda fucking nightmare, I bet."

"Shut up," Derrick growled, fingers fisting around his beer until he'd crushed the cup in lieu of crushing that asshole's fucking face.

Maybe they hadn't heard him, 'cos they kept talking.

"I don't believe for one second that a chick could do stunts like that."

"Yeah? You think they got a guy doubling for the Black Widow? Moron."

"Think he still likes dick?"

"Shut up," Derrick said again, louder this time. Much louder. Too loud. "I said *shut up*!"

The whole tent went silent, except for the buzz of *Wolf's Landing* in the background. Derrick realized he was on his feet, both hands fisted, sticky beer cup still crushed in his left. Everyone was staring at him. *Everyone*, and God help him he felt twelve again, cornered on the school playground while bullies taunted him about two queens and his little French maid's dress. He wanted to flee. He wanted to punch these fuckers in the face. He wanted to bury his shameful fucking head in the sand because he hadn't even told these guys—told *anyone*—he was *gay*, while Ginsberg had been brave enough, strong enough, tough enough to have announced to the whole fucking world that he was queer *and* trans and then go get run over by cars for a living.

Ginsberg hadn't been trying to *change* Derrick. He'd just been trying to get Derrick to be his own fucking *self*, and not the man his father had thought he should be or his old classmates thought he should be or these loggers thought he should be or even that he himself had mistakenly thought he should be. To embrace himself. To be *happy*.

But Ginsberg was right. Derrick *was* a coward. Had been his whole fucking life. And what had it gotten him but shitty beer and terrible company out in the ass end of the world.

All that terrible company was still staring at him. He met their eyes, one at a time. Tossed his cup in the trash. "*I* like dick," he said. "Anyone got a problem with that, I'll be in my trailer."

Which he then left for, stunned silence in his wake.

Maybe, just *maybe*, it wasn't too late to fix things after all.

As Derrick threw his clothes into his duffel, he ran over and over in his head what he might say. Winning Ginsberg back was *not* going to be easy, he knew that. He'd fucked up so bad he couldn't blame the kid if he stayed away forever. Fuck, they hadn't even spoken in a month; for all he knew, Ginsberg might've met someone else in the meanwhile.

It was no surprise, then, that Ginsberg didn't answer the phone when Derrick called. The first time, or the second time, or the third time.

At which point Derrick stopped trying and just headed home, instead.

Because what he *did* know for sure was that if he had any hope of convincing Ginsberg he'd changed, he needed to prove it to himself first.

So back to the B&B he went, only stopping for groceries along the way. When he got home, despite the cold, he opened every window for a good few hours to let the place air out while he changed all the old sheets and towels he hadn't bothered to strip from the guest rooms before he'd left. Laundry next, and a hard scrubbing in the kitchen, including the petri dish the fridge had become. Once he'd closed the windows, he lit the fireplace in the common room and sat down with his computer, determined to figure out how to get the website back up and registrations reopened. He spent a good three hours dealing with all the third-party sites that listed hotel rooms—the ones Ginsberg had showed him how to use, go figure—and then he took a shower, changed into presentable clothes, and headed into the kitchen to cook himself a decent meal.

First, though, he fished the pink donut apron out of his living room trash.

Didn't even feel silly putting it on. Just . . . sad and determined.

When the tears came halfway through chopping vegetables, he didn't even try to pretend they were because of the onion. Men cried when their hearts were broken. That was okay. He was damn well fucking allowed.

He dried his eyes on his apron and finished his meal. It was getting late, but he took a last pass through the old house, dusting and straightening. He realized he didn't mind the work at all. Had even kind of enjoyed the cooking, brief bout of sobbing excluded. Besides, everything needed to be absolutely *perfect* for what was to come.

Ginsberg deserved no less.

The quiet of the empty house seemed downright oppressive after the noise and life of the logging camp, and even more so after the noise and life that Ginsberg had once brought to these rooms and halls. He missed having the kid in his bed. He missed having the kid in his *life*.

But he slept, and if he dreamed he didn't remember, and he woke up in the morning more determined than ever.

The first thing he did was check his phone for messages. Ginsberg hadn't called or texted, but he didn't let that deter him. He almost gave in and tried calling again, but talked himself out of it. It was futile, and Ginsberg deserved better than to feel like his ex was stalking him.

He checked his email instead, breath held against the hope that maybe someone had booked a stay. He wouldn't have nearly as much time to wallow if the rooms were filled with guests. There was nothing yet, but that was okay. He'd probably upset a lot of people by canceling all those reservations without any notice last month. He decided that when he got home tonight, he'd write each and every one of them a personal apology and offer them a night on the house. Maybe some would take him up on it. Maybe some would even stay an extra few days.

But he couldn't waste time on that right now. No, it was already 8 a.m., and Ginsberg would surely be on set soon, if not already.

Down in the kitchen, he made himself a straight black coffee and a sausage omelet, put his dishes in the dishwasher, and then headed out. He had his keys in his hand and his fingers on the front doorknob before he realized he'd forgotten one very important thing, and ran back into the kitchen to grab it. Then he hopped in his truck and headed off to the sprawling *Wolf's Landing* set on the north edge of town.

He had a man to win back, after all.

"I'm sorry sir but you can't just walk onto the set."

Derrick groaned. "Please. C'mon. I'm local. I don't have a criminal record. I just need to talk to Ginsberg Sloan. You know Ginsberg Sloan?"

The rent-a-cop gave his head a shake. "Sure, but do you think I would get to keep my job if I let every name-dropping fan waltz onto the set?"

"But I'm not a fan! I don't even watch the show. Or, well, I do now but I didn't a week ago."

". . . Right."

"Please, look, I gotta see Ginsberg. You can even escort me. Or you can call him! I have his number, see?" He fished his phone from his pocket, scrolled to Ginsberg's name and held it up. The rent-a-cop didn't bother to look, so Derrick waved it in front of his face. "You can call him. Or you can page him on your walkie-talkie or however it is you guys get ahold of each other here. He'll vouch for me."

I hope.

"Sorry, buddy, no can do. If you really want onto the set, you can sign up for a tour like everybody else. Costs thirty-five bucks and starts at 10 a.m. Keep your hands inside the cart at all times or we'll be talking again a lot less friendly."

This was friendly? Derrick sighed.

"And just a word of advice: next time you try to walk onto a closed set? Maybe you'll have better luck convincing security you're not a crazy person if you're not wearing . . . that."

Derrick looked down at himself and sighed. Okay, yeah, he had to admit the guy had a point, but what did it say about the world they lived in that it was even an issue in the first place?

He mustered up a smile from somewhere, mostly because he realized that *Ginsberg* had taught him to think like that. "Sure, buddy. Thanks. So, where's the ticket office?"

"Back the way you came, swing a left on the ring road, follow it down to the far side of the back lot. You'll see a little gift shop and a couple of trams. Who knows, maybe you'll get real lucky and Ginsberg will sign your . . . outfit."

Maybe, if he got real lucky, Ginsberg would do way more.

CHAPTER TWENTY

Eventually, Ginsberg just turned his phone off.

Not because Derrick's repeated phone calls were scary or even annoying, but more because the longer he camped out in guest rooms—even if it was a very nice guest room in a very nice mansion—the lonelier and more dejected he got and the harder it was to keep himself from answering.

He wasn't going to fucking answer. He *wasn't.*

The loneliness would pass. So would the near homelessness, even if he would be spending yet another Thanksgiving and Christmas in someone else's place. He didn't need an asshole like Derrick to fix those problems, the same as he didn't need his parents to fix them, either. Better to be in a friend's guest room than in a toxic but stable living situation. Because toxic *wasn't* stable.

His therapist had told him that years ago, and it was as true now as it'd been back then.

And yet somehow he couldn't quite believe that the man who had made love to him with such attention and care, who'd cooked with him and cleaned with him and even shaved with him on occasion, who'd made everything about their relationship so utterly *normal,* could be toxic.

And yet here we are.

The guy had been a good actor, that was all. Maybe Ginsberg could suggest him for a part. Nah, any Hollywood position obviously wouldn't pass his manliness test. Unless they were filming *The Expendables 17* out in the deep wilderness, or something.

He still found himself with his phone in his hand between takes. Off, but in his hand. After like the thirtieth time, he forced himself to put it back on his chair, flexed his arm and went through a quick stretching routine before they called him back in for Levi's coverage. He needed to stay focused on the scene if he didn't want to get hurt again. He still hadn't built back all the muscle in his arm, and shooting the same stunt three times in a row from three different angles wasn't doing it any favors. At least he had twenty minutes between each reset to enjoy the weather; it wasn't usually this nice in November, and he'd been spending so much time indoors lately that shooting on the back lot was a rare treat. The sunlight was doing wonders for his mood. In fact, maybe instead of sitting around with his phone, he could go for a brisk walk instead. He hopped out of his seat.

"Where you headed off to?" Levi asked from the seat in front of him.

"Clear my head."

Levi pointed significantly to his watch. "It's *almost ten*."

Oh, joy. Just what he needed—to be caught out by the fucking *tour* bus. Like the studio didn't make enough money from this show already? They had to bring gawking fans onto set once a day too? Not that they were gawking for Ginsberg, but he was dressed like Carter today, complete with the stupid wig, so the likelihood of mistaken identity was too high to ignore.

"Fine." He sighed and plopped back in his seat.

"Speaking of, I'll be in my trailer," Levi said with a wink, but Melanie materialized over his shoulder and pushed him back down. "We're reset in five. Stay right here."

"I'll stay and keep you company," Ginsberg offered. They almost had the new window hung for him to crash through, anyway.

The tour bus—which was in fact a rickety golf cart towing a couple passenger trams—arrived right on cue. Levi visibly bristled.

"Places!" Melanie called, and Levi and Ginsberg moved to their marks. From the tram speakers came the familiar refrain of, "Ooh, look how lucky we are today—they're about to shoot a scene! We'll take some time and pause here so you can watch, but everyone needs to stay very, very quiet and make sure their phones are off, okay? And remember, for the safety of our performers, absolutely no videotaping or flash photography."

The whole crew seemed to change somehow, aware that the performance had taken on another level. As snide as an antisocial hermit like Levi could be, everyone (him included) knew these were the people responsible for their livelihoods. The superfans who kept them in the consciousness of social media, who created reams of cool and weird and weird/cool fan works that did a better job of recruiting new viewers than even the best-planned ad campaign. That tram was their equivalent of a live studio audience, and it was their job to make them happy.

But of course, despite the best efforts of the tour guide, every so often someone on the tram couldn't contain their hysteria, and today was one of those days.

A male voice, starting in a mutter but escalating to a yell. Which meant poor Levi would probably have to loop the whole scene later.

"Ginsberg Sloan!" the fan from the tram called.

Well that was new. Nobody ever called for *his* attention.

It distracted him just enough that he missed his cue, and Levi's perfectly timed and executed fake punch turned into a real one instead, half-pulled at the last instant but still clocking him right on the damn jaw. He stumbled back, clutching his face, as Levi sputtered apologies.

Security practically dragged a bristling Levi off the set as the medic came to check Ginsberg's face and the tour guide's microphone hummed to life: "—remind everyone to please be quiet and stay seated and— No, sir, you need to stay on the— *Sir*—"

The next thing Ginsberg knew, a big lumbering shape was jumping off the tram and running full tilt in his direction, trying to beat the remaining set security, who were converging from all directions.

Ginsberg shook off the medic's probing fingers, stood, and gaped, too shocked to do anything else. Not like he had practice dodging crazed fans like some of the other show regulars.

And then his dazed eyes caught a glimpse of pink.

A pink-and-yellow apron, frilly and printed with a pattern of happy little donuts.

And wearing it was . . . Derrick.

Right at the moment of realization, security and Derrick collided in a veritable explosion of muscular men, and somebody let out a shrill scream.

"Please!" Derrick's voice broke through the commotion.

At some point, a guard had moved in front of Ginsberg, a wall of bodybuilder protecting him.

"Just wanna talk to you!" Derrick yelled. "Ginsberg!"

Ginsberg looked around, not sure whether he was more excited and flattered or fucking humiliated. If not for that pink apron, he'd have probably fallen squarely on the side of humiliated, but as it was . . .

Security had Derrick by the upper arms and were dragging him bodily away, his heels scraping through the dirt.

The tour tram had puttered off for less-exciting pastures.

If this were a movie, security would have asked Ginsberg what he wanted to do with the guy, but this wasn't a movie, and every five minutes of unplanned downtime cost the production like a thousand bucks, and Derrick with his frilly pink apron and his shouting and his struggling seemed insane, so they were getting the threat off the premises immediately. Lawyers were probably being called. Maybe even police. Ginsberg likely wouldn't be consulted until after the day's shooting, when the studio tried to decide what kind of charges to press and damages to seek. That was the way these things went. There was a procedure. Everyone on set, right down to the PAs on coffee runs, knew that.

"I'm sorry!" Derrick yelled.

"Little late for that," one of the security guys quipped.

Ginsberg knew he should say the same.

"I made a terrible mistake! Ginsberg—" They were dragging him further and further away, and still he was struggling. "Ginsberg, listen! I was afraid, okay? I was so afraid of not being man enough that it made me stupid! I was so scared, but you—" A brief tangle of arms and legs as Derrick dug his heels in to prevent security from pulling him out of earshot. "You were brave! And you were more of a man—"

Ah, *fuck*.

Set procedure be damned, Ginsberg chased after them.

Somehow, he convinced them to let Derrick go, marched Derrick over to his chair without a word—though Derrick had plenty, wouldn't stop apologizing for five fucking seconds—and sat him down with a harsh point of his finger. "Be quiet. Stay here. In case you didn't notice, I am *working*." But then he felt awful at Derrick's kicked-puppy face, so strange on a man that age and size and level of grizzle, and added, softer, "We'll talk after, okay? Just . . . wait."

Ginsberg apologized to cast and crew nearly as profusely as Derrick had to him, and then managed to finish shooting all the coverage on the stupid window-throw scene without getting hurt. Once more through the fight, once more through the glass, and then they were done with him for the next eighty minutes.

Derrick was wide-eyed and fidgety when Ginsberg collected him from his chair and walked him to his trailer. Ginsberg sat them down on the couch, folded his arms, and said, "Okay. Talk."

For a guy who hadn't stopped shouting even with security bruising his arms, Derrick was sure lost for words now. He stared at Ginsberg awhile, giving him big watery blinks, then sighed. "I'm sorry, Ginsberg. I'm sorry for how I treated you and the things I said and the things I did. I was wrong about absolutely everything. *Everything.*"

"Well, thanks for saying so, and yes, you were." Ginsberg kept his arms crossed. He didn't give the guy anything else.

Derrick floundered in the frosty silence, and finally managed, "Where are . . . where are you staying?"

"Thanks to you? At Carter and Levi's. I get a guest room, at least. I'm getting too old and have too bad of a neck for couchsurfing anymore."

"Have you ever . . ." Derrick gulped. "Have you ever even had a place of your own?"

Ginsberg almost considered not telling him—*You don't deserve to know anything about me*—but then he decided the truth would hurt Derrick more than letting the guy think that everything was okay. "Too many bills and not enough work to pay them and afford a house. Too *much* work to settle down anywhere even if I could afford it; it was always LA to Vancouver to LA to Vancouver and then finally to here. And no family home to fall back on, either. Just me and my bike and my duffel bag."

"You never even had anywhere to come home to?"

You, his traitorous brain supplied, and he surprised them both when his mouth said, "I did, once. For a little while, until *someone* ruined everything."

Silence hung heavy and awkward after that. Long enough for Ginsberg to think about making Derrick leave.

But then Derrick blurted, "I came out at work."

Huh? "I thought you closed the B&B down."

"No, I mean— Yes, I did, but then I took a camp job. Logging," he added at Ginsberg's confusion.

"Passed your manhood test, did it?"

"I thought it did," Derrick replied. "Until I up and realized the test was wrong. That even *having* a test was wrong."

Don't hope don't hope don't hope . . . But of course he couldn't help asking, "Is that what you meant when you said you were scared stupid and I was . . . brave?"

He nodded. "I was always so afraid that people would find out I really was gay, especially since everyone *already* called me a girl for working in the B&B. But I understand now that being a man means being brave enough to know that manhood can't be measured that way. *You* taught me that."

"Did you rehearse that speech?"

For the first time, a tiny, nervous smile fractured Derrick's panicked face. "No. Jim came up with it."

Ginsberg didn't know whether to laugh or hit the guy again. "He told you what to say to me?"

"Not exactly. More like, he yelled it in my ear *at* me."

"And then?"

"And then I offered him a full-time job at the B&B and use of the kitchen if he wants to do catering or online orders or something for more business."

That . . . wow. Ginsberg needed a second to digest that. Derrick had reopened the B&B? And more importantly, "You guys made up, then?"

"Not exactly. He said he'd only take the job if you were there."

Ginsberg ground his teeth, stupid, inexplicable tears burning the backs of his eyes. Was *that* what this was about? All this trouble to reopen the stupid Baywater-Bayview-Baywhatever B&B? "You *kicked me out*."

Derrick somehow looked more sheepish than ever. "Yeah, I did. But you know what, I realized something. That place is as much yours now as it ever was mine. I had no right to kick you out. None at all." He reached into his pocket, dug around a little, and retrieved a key on a ring. "This is yours. I want you to sign a joint ownership agreement. Even if you just take a part of the profits. Or if you like running the place but you don't want me around, I guess I could go back to camp and stay outta your and Jim's hair. Just . . . whatever makes you happy, okay? But for what it's worth, I want you to *come home*."

The tears gathered force, spilled right down his face, no doubt streaking his makeup. Suyin was going to kill him, but it was hard to care just now, torn between two extremes as he was. On the one hand, Derrick . . . wow, just . . . *wow*, Derrick was offering him half the B&B? For *nothing*? Willing to leave, even, just to make him happy?

On the other hand, Derrick had been a colossal ass, and if Ginsberg had learned anything from his past relationships, it was *once bitten, twice shy*.

But on the *other* other hand, Derrick was *offering him half the B&B*.

He . . . didn't know what to feel. Except kind of like that guy in that Tumblr GIF, spinning in circles on the floor and screaming *My whole brain is crying!*

When he opened his mouth to speak, he legitimately had no idea what was about to come out of it. "I can't quit my job, Derrick. And I won't be in Bluewater Bay forever. That hasn't changed. Somebody calls me to work on the next Marvel movie, I'm gonna be off to Budapest playing Hawkeye in a hot second."

"So you hire a manager to run the place when you're not around. Or I do it. You gotta come home from playing Hawkeye sometime. I want this to be your home. I want you to have it. *Please*."

"That's *all* you want?" Ginsberg asked. The words felt as tender as a bruise, as tender as his newly healed bones.

"Well, no. *I* want to be your home too. But I don't have any right to ask you that after how I acted." He held out the key again, urged Ginsberg to take it. "So let's just start with this."

Ginsberg hiccuped. His wet eyes leaked. He wanted so badly to reach out. His body itched. His fingers flexed. "You ever gonna take that apron off?" he asked, because if he didn't joke about *something* he was going to fall to the ground bawling.

Derrick looked down at himself with a crooked grin. Toyed with the ruffles on his lap. "Not until you take this damn key. I'll wear it back to camp if I have to."

"You really mean that."

Derrick's gaze locked on his own, eyes shining. The crooked smile faded. "Yeah. I do. I've been a coward all my life, Ginsberg. Closeted and afraid to cry and afraid to ever commit to my swishy twink ex-boyfriend who was so damn good to me my whole damn life, and afraid to succeed or even try at my business and then you showed up and I was so damn afraid to be honest with you that I betrayed your trust." He took a deep breath. "And then, even worse, once I *didn't* want to kick you out, I was afraid to just . . . love you. Well, I'm not being a coward anymore. If I can't have you back, then I'm at least gonna use the time I spent with you—the time you gave to me—to learn to be a better man."

Oh hell. What was he supposed to *do* with that?

And had Derrick just . . . "You *love* me?"

Derrick laughed, explosive and quick. "I am crying in a pink apron in the middle of a Hollywood-transplant film set while trying to give half my house away. Yes, I'd say that qualifies. I love you. I *love you*. And you don't have to love me back, but it won't change the way I feel about you." He snatched up Ginsberg's hand, firm but gentle, uncurled Ginsberg's fingers and pressed the key into his palm. "Come home, Ginsberg. Please."

Ginsberg might still be angry, and the two of them still had a lot of talking and a lot of work to do, but really, there was only one way to reply to that: Ginsberg leaned in and kissed his forehead. "Okay," he said. "But if I'm gonna part own this place, we're changing the name."

Derrick sat back just far enough to meet Ginsberg's eyes. They were both sniffling through tears, but there was no mistaking the relief, the joy on Derrick's face. "The Man Cave?"

"Eeeeeh." Ginsberg matched Derrick's crooked smile with one of his own. "We'll work on it."

They'd have to work on a *lot* of things. Ginsberg knew that. But now that they were working toward the same goal, he had faith they'd get there.

CHAPTER TWENTY-ONE

The Burnt Toast B&B, said the banner at the top of Ginsberg's newly redesigned website.

"Because I'm a bad cook?" Derrick asked, scrunching his nose. That struck him as a *terrible* idea. "Won't that scare people off?"

"I think it's cute," Jim put in. "Just like you two."

Ginsberg did an overexaggerated gag. "Stop trying to matchmake us, Jim. If it's gonna happen, it'll happen."

"Yes, with a little interference from your favorite employee."

"You're our *only* employee," Derrick grumbled.

"And your favorite."

"*A-ny-way.* Back to the name. I like it," Ginsberg said.

"Of course you do. You came up with it."

"It's quirky, it speaks to you as a person, it's memorable—everything the old name wasn't."

"But it implies that I burn the food. And considering we're selling lunch and dinner now too, that's . . . not gonna pay Jim's salary?"

"But you *do* burn the food. That's why you hired me." Jim nudged Derrick with his elbow.

"If you really don't like it, we can go back to the drawing board," Ginsberg said, sounding more dejected than Derrick could stand. Which was actually a pretty low bar to cross, if he was being honest.

"No, no. You're part owner now. You handle the image stuff. You like it, I like it."

Jim made a whipping sound. And did the action.

"We're not dating," Ginsberg reminded him through his teeth.

But behind the faux annoyance, Derrick could see as clear as anything that he was pleased.

"Okay," he said. "Here goes nothing. We put this up, then we send out the free night's stay emails, and that's it. We're in business."

He hit publish.

And somewhere around the fifty percent loaded mark, Ginsberg covertly took his hand.

Two months later, they reached a dizzying milestone: including Ginsberg's, every single room in the B&B was booked for the entire weekend. A few of the rooms were even occupied by the jilted guests Derrick had begged to give them a second chance. But this time, they were paying customers. Ginsberg couldn't have been prouder—of the business *or* of Derrick, who hadn't once lapsed back into his old toxic behavior.

No, he was much too busy pining after Ginsberg like a lovesick puppy for that. And damn the man, but Ginsberg felt himself growing weaker and weaker each day in the face of it.

Fortunately, though, he had a ton of work to throw himself into. The bed-and-breakfast bits of the business weren't the only parts thriving. Jim sold out of his $20-a-plate lunches and $30-a-plate dinners daily (fine wines and gourmet desserts extra, of course), drawing significant extra revenue for the B&B (and making almost equally significant extra work for all of them), and right now he was busy in the kitchen baking three hundred cupcakes for an upcoming hipster wedding.

The house party Ginsberg and Derrick had put on with the Stomping Grounds back when the B&B had still been called *BaySomething* had been such a success that tonight they'd hosted another one solo, this time with a wine tasting and an honest-to-God harpist.

Ginsberg felt terrible about having skipped out on setup—the *Wolf's Landing* shooting schedule was nonnegotiable and he'd been stuck on set till almost nine—but he was back now and making up for lost time picking up the hundreds of plastic wine glasses their guest sommelier had asked them to provide. Apparently his fee didn't include taking that shit to the recycling, but hey, even minus the cost to have him and the harpist in, they were still way ahead, money they were planning on using to install a gorgeous expensive convection oven for Jim.

As a surprise, of course, because Derrick was nothing if not a complete cheeseball.

He kept giving Ginsberg dumb little smiles every time their gazes met and lovesick sighs every time he thought Ginsberg *wasn't* looking. And the frilly pink apron that had become his signature—mentioned in nearly every online review—looked weirdly hot tied so tightly at the base of his broad back.

Not that Ginsberg was looking at him that way.

(Ginsberg was totally looking at him that way.)

Derrick started running the vacuum as Ginsberg gathered up the last of the plastic cups and wiped down every horizontal surface on the ground floor, which all guests had a remarkable talent for leaving weird and sticky. It was late and he was tired—he'd left the house at 6 a.m. to hit morning call, and had spent nine straight hours shooting about thirty seconds of a fight scene. But his gaze kept straying to Derrick as he cleaned. Sometimes to his butt, showcased beneath the ties of the apron. Sometimes to his darting eyes and nervous smile. Most times to all of him at once, somehow, just . . . staring and staring and staring.

Ginsberg sighed and fell into the nearest chair. It was time. Even *he* couldn't keep pretending that he wasn't utterly smitten.

Derrick had called him the bigger man, the brave one, the fearless one, but he was wrong. In fact, Ginsberg felt like just as much of a coward right now as he'd *ever* accused Derrick of being. Because all he could think about was how much he *wanted* this, how much it meant to him, how much he was growing (okay, had grown; horse, barn door, etc., etc.) to love Derrick again—and how badly he might be hurt again because of it. Even though Derrick had done *nothing* in the past month to indicate he might hurt Ginsberg, and *everything* in the past month to indicate he wouldn't. He wasn't a changed man, but he *had* become an enlightened one. A better version of himself than he'd ever been.

So why was Ginsberg so afraid to take that final step again?

Once bitten, twice shy, bucko.

Except . . . it would have to be him. With Derrick's enlightenment had come an understanding that he couldn't pressure Ginsberg, only wait. And Ginsberg appreciated that: appreciated the time and the respect and the space.

But damn was it hard to break the pattern.

The vacuum switched off, plunging the room into silence. The overnight guests had gone to bed, or out on the town for an extra-late night.

"So," Derrick said, standing in the doorway and rubbing the back of his neck. "I think we're all done here."

"Yeah," Ginsberg said, tying a knot in his blue bag full of cups. "Can you run these to the recycling depot tomorrow?"

Derrick nodded. His ears were red. Had he had a couple drinks, too?

No, judging by the shuffling of his feet, he was just embarrassed and blushing.

"Yeah, so, um, thanks for helping out, you know? I know you had a long day on set."

Ginsberg fiddled with the ends on the recycling bag, shrugging one shoulder. "S'nothing. Just spent nine hours getting the tar beaten out of me. Piece of cake."

Derrick's laugh obviously caught him by surprise—he practically barked like a seal. "S'crazy is what it is. You're insane. Do you, um . . ." He dropped his eyes to his feet, cleared his throat. The red flush had spread all the way up to his hairline and down past his collar. "Maybe need a massage, or anything?"

Oh. That was a pickup line, wasn't it? It *sounded* like a pickup line? But Derrick looked so little-boy earnest he legitimately couldn't tell.

"I'm pretty sure I'm only allowed to get massages from vetted professionals," he said, only half-joking. "Besides, they bring a guy on set. He comes in for a couple hours every day 'cos we all spend so much time getting our asses kicked."

"Oh! Oh, yeah. No shit. Guess they don't want you going to any bargain basement chiropractors and breaking your back."

"Exactly," Ginsberg said with a little laugh.

God, why couldn't he have just taken the fucking opening?

They stood in silence for a painfully long time, until Derrick finally said, "It was a great party."

"Looked like it, yeah."

"Do you, uh . . ." Derrick was staring up at the ceiling, suddenly. "Do you remember the last party we had here?"

"Of . . . course?" Ginsberg replied.

"Remember . . . after?"

Ginsberg's face went hot. Derrick's fingers and cock stuffing him full. Derrick's wet mouth on his dick. "Yeah," he breathed.

"You, uh," Derrick rubbed his arm and shuffled his feet. His pecs looked downright yummy bunched up the way they were what with him hugging himself. But it was his face, the earnest emotion there, that was selling Ginsberg. "You wanna maybe, uh, do that again?"

Good question: did he? Poor Derrick looked braced for a punch to the face or worse, and was making no attempt to hide his nerves, his vulnerability. It was all there on display for Ginsberg to see—to do with what he would—and if that wasn't brave as fuck, then Ginsberg didn't know the meaning of the word.

It was well past time for Ginsberg to be brave again in return.

He held out his hand. "Yeah. Yeah, I think I do."

"Oh, wow," Derrick said with a gasp. "I thought I was gonna have to offer to let you top before you'd even *consider* saying yes."

Ginsberg's eyebrows shot up. Unenlightened Derrick would've never deigned to be the bottom. Women and fairies were the ones who bottomed in Unenlightened Derrick's world. "*Are* you offering?" he asked with a smile.

"Not if you don't want to. I mean, I was just thinking. I was thinking how you said that you can use your packer to fuck guys with. Thinking maybe you could fuck me with it too. If you, um. Wanted to."

"Were they sexy thoughts?" Ginsberg slunk close and traced a finger down the center of Derrick's pink donut–covered chest, right down the dip between his pecs.

It seemed the power of speech had fled the man, because he just grunted kind of confusedly and nodded.

Ginsberg took his hand and tugged him toward Derrick's private rooms. "Have you ever . . .?" he asked as they passed through the kitchen.

Derrick stopped. Shook his head. Started pulling him back toward the common room and up the stairs. "No. I mean yes. I mean, once. A long time ago. Senior year. We went to Seattle for spring break with a fistful of quarters and fake IDs. Older guy bought me some drinks. Big logger type." Derrick shrugged, blushing again. "It was flattering, you know? I wasn't out at home. I let him take me for a spin later that night. Told my friends he was . . . actually, I don't remember what lie I told them about him. Maybe that he was gonna get me some hash and didn't have room in his car for anyone else."

This night was getting more and more interesting by the second. "Did you like it?" Ginsberg asked.

Derrick shrugged again. "Wasn't really my thing, no. I mean, he didn't hurt me too bad or anything, but . . . No. But after everything that happened with you these last couple months, I'm wondering if maybe it was all in my head. Like maybe my body would like it if my insecurities didn't get in the way."

"Did Jim tell you that, too?"

"What can I say," Derrick said with a vulnerable little shrug and an even more vulnerable smile. "Guy's *smart*."

For the first time in over two months, Ginsberg got up on his tiptoes and kissed Derrick on the lips.

Except this time, the kiss was different. There were no more secrets between them now. No more lies, no more resentment, no more toxic beliefs, no more lingering disrespect or mistrust. They shared everything now.

And sharing made it all so much better.

Including this.

Ginsberg felt like he was undressing in front of Derrick for the first time. He wasn't nervous, or afraid of what Derrick would think, just . . . it all felt fresh, exciting, somehow *new*. He wanted to tease and tantalize, wanted to reveal every part of himself one slow inch at a time while Derrick's hungry gaze tried to devour him whole.

He felt *powerful*.

Conversely, vulnerability came off of Derrick in waves as he sat there on the edge of the bed—Ginsberg's bed, and there was something beautifully significant about Derrick having insisted they do this in Ginsberg's space, on his home turf—still in his stupid apron. Not insecurity the way he used to express it, but a healthier, more open form. A state of being that had him saying, "I'm a little nervous, so go easy on me, okay?"

Ginsberg appreciated that. It was brave to ask for this, but braver still to admit he wasn't one hundred percent confident and in control. Ginsberg could get him there.

Buck naked now, he strode over to Derrick, climbed into his lap and kissed him. Derrick moaned into his mouth like Ginsberg was that first gulp of beer on a hot summer day, hand looping around Ginsberg's waist and sliding up his bare back. Their groins were touching, but neither of them sought friction. Not yet. Instead Ginsberg slid his hands down Derrick's shoulders, back, to his waist, and untied the apron string.

"Let's get you undressed," he murmured against Derrick's lips.

Derrick nodded, but he still chased after Ginsberg's mouth when Ginsberg shifted off his lap to unbutton his dress shirt. He froze as Ginsberg worked, eyes closed and chin tilted up and lips parted and reaching, just waiting for Ginsberg to come back.

Instead Ginsberg pushed the shirt off Derrick's shoulders, then lifted the hem of his undershirt and tugged it over his head. Ran his fingernails through Derrick's chest hair and raked them across his nipples so that he gasped. Lowered himself to his aching knees on the floor at Derrick's feet and stripped him from the waist down, too.

Nervous as Derrick admittedly was, he was still rock hard, and Ginsberg took the opportunity to give his dick a few rewarding strokes. His mouth watered, but he was saving his tongue for bigger and better things, so for now he stuck with his hand. Derrick didn't touch him back, but that was okay; Ginsberg got more than enough pleasure watching Derrick, palms planted on the mattress, head tipped back in pleasure.

"Turn over," Ginsberg directed. "On your hands and knees."

"A-already?" Derrick yelped.

"Yes," Ginsberg said firmly, but with a smile. "I *already* want you on your hands and knees. Not gonna fuck you yet though. Or at all, if you change your mind."

"Not changing my mind," Derrick grumbled, like a petulant child.

"Good. Hands and knees, then."

His in-charge tone and Derrick's quick acquiescence had him thinking of Jim and his whipping sounds.

Derrick was trembling as he got on his hands and knees, baring his ass. Ginsberg stroked and petted him, touching his sides and thighs as soothingly as he could manage.

"We'll take it slow. Just like you did for me."

Starting with his tongue, just like Derrick had.

"Get a move on," Derrick griped.

Ginsberg kissed, then gently bit, Derrick's left ass cheek. Petted him more. Ginsberg was a bit of a masochist himself—let's face it, all stuntmen were—but he didn't know yet what Derrick liked or how hard he'd want it. Best to err on the side of caution, make him feel as safe as he'd made Ginsberg feel during their one night together.

But it was a gentle touch—the first swipe of his tongue over Derrick's hole—that actually startled Derrick.

"Whoa, whoa, whoa," he complained, ass cheeks clamping tight together.

"Don't like it?" Ginsberg asked carefully.

"Well I didn't say that. But . . ."

"But what?" Ginsberg crouched on the floor, rubbing Derrick's thighs absently.

"But you don't have to do that kind of thing. Not to *me*."

"Because you don't like it?"

"No!"

"Then what? You were okay doing it for me. If you don't like it, that's okay, but if it's something else . . ."

Derrick dropped his head onto his forearms, but left his ass in the air, and was silent for a long moment before mumbling, "It's just I'm not used to anyone paying that much attention to me, is all. I've never . . ." significant pause ". . . you know? And it's kind of . . ."

"Self-conscious?" Ginsberg tried.

Derrick nodded into his arms.

"But you don't mind getting head. S'not really any different, is it?"

Another long pause. "I guess not . . .?"

There was of course one other explanation, one Ginsberg was praying to every deity under the sun wasn't true. "This doesn't have anything to do with feeling . . . emasculated, does it?"

"What?" Derrick popped back up on both hands and jerked his head around to meet Ginsberg's gaze over his shoulder. "No! No. It's not that at all, it's . . . You know what? Just shut up and get back to work."

There was no mistaking the good-natured mischief behind all the blushing gruffness, so Ginsberg put it all down to nerves and self-consciousness and just plain newness after all, and tried again.

Derrick was stiff, but that didn't last long. No more than a minute in, he was out of his mind moaning, making high, needy noises Ginsberg had never heard come out of his mouth before.

Fuck, he was into it. If this was Derrick's sexual self from here on out, Ginsberg was never leaving him ever. He lapped and prodded and swirled in turns, holding Derrick by the hips to keep him from squirming away.

And yeah, he was squirming. Not the get-off-me-I-hate-this kind of squirming, but the this-is-so-good-I-can-barely-stand-it kind.

That day Derrick had nearly gotten himself arrested on set, he'd apologized for abusing Ginsberg's trust. For making him feel homeless, lost, threatened, out of control of his own fate.

Right here, right now, with Derrick a helpless, panting mess beneath him? He couldn't have felt those things any *less* if he'd tried. Because back then, Derrick had held all the power, all the control, and he hadn't used it at all. And now he'd wrapped it up in a little box with ribbons and bows and handed it to Ginsberg on bended knee. No question Ginsberg was in charge here tonight, no question about the security of Ginsberg's place in this house and in Derrick's heart, and no question either that reserved, stoic Derrick had finally, *finally* laid himself bare, just as vulnerable as Ginsberg had ever been.

"Even Steven," he announced, pulling out of his assault so he could pat Derrick on the ass. "Lube and condom's in the bedside drawer."

"R-right," Derrick breathed, sounding way more turned on and dazed than nervous now. Right where Ginsberg wanted him.

"Grab the felt bag, too."

Derrick nodded and leaned forward to reach into the nightstand, then returned to his position and pressed the bottle of lube, a condom, and the felt bag into Ginsberg's waiting hand.

Ginsberg pulled the harness and erection rod from the felt bag, wedged the rod into his packer to make it hard and then strapped it on with the harness to make sure he wouldn't lose it at a particularly inopportune time. Then he slicked up his fingers and rolled a condom down the packer, enjoying how fat and firm the silicone felt with the rod inside it. "One last chance to back out," he said.

"Never," Derrick replied, huffing and whimpering as Ginsberg worked a finger and then two inside him. No real need for more prep; he was wet and loose already from the rimming, but Ginsberg couldn't resist going directly for his prostate with a couple of fingertips.

"N-never—*Oh*! Never backing out. This is it for me, you hear? *You're* it for me. You leave me now, I'm gonna die horny and alone."

He was making a joke, but the sincerity behind it brought tears to Ginsberg's eyes.

This is it.

Us. Forever.

Yes.

God only knew why he'd waited so damn long.

No trace of hesitance left, he pushed forward, taking Derrick in one slow, even stroke.

Sliding *home.*

Derrick lay sleepy and sated in the aftermath of that *amazing* fuck. He felt boneless like a jellyfish, and slimy like one too. He squirmed in Ginsberg's arms. Ginsberg, in turn, just tightened his grip and kissed Derrick's ear. "You'll get up and wash your ass when I'm ready to let you go, and not one second earlier."

"You're planning on falling asleep with me like this," Derrick complained, but had to admit he didn't actually mind . . . much. He felt way too good. The aftershocks had mostly faded, but . . . wow. Just . . . *wow*. He was pretty sure he'd never come so hard in his life, and if he were being very honest with himself, that hadn't even been the best part.

No, the *best* part was the man behind him, currently holding him hostage.

Ginsberg laughed, the heat of his breath on Derrick's nape undeniably sexy. Sexy enough to be considering another round, even though Derrick was sticky front and back. He could overlook it. He really could.

"Alright, I'll take mercy on you since you were such a good sport." Ginsberg's arm lifted from Derrick's shoulder, letting him free. "Aren't you glad you moved me to a room with its own shower?"

Derrick chuckled, picturing himself streaking naked down the third-floor hallway with a house full of guests. Then realized that getting up at all was the last thing he wanted. He pulled Ginsberg's arm back around his shoulders. "I changed my mind. I stay, you stay."

Ginsberg sighed and snuggled back in. "I was hoping you'd say that."

"Hoping I'd let you leach more heat from me despite my sloppy . . ." *ass*? he didn't say, because he suddenly felt bashful about the whole thing all over again.

"Hoping you'd ask me to stay," Ginsberg corrected, his voice soft.

"Please stay with me," Derrick said, because he wanted to make it official. "Here. For as long as you can. And when you have to leave, come home to me too?"

"You got it, baby." Ginsberg hummed with pleasure, and Derrick felt a matching warmth in his chest, one he'd never felt in his life before. One he'd never let himself feel before he'd let Ginsberg into his home and his heart. "But if I'm staying, I should probably move into your suite with you, open up *this* room for guests. But if I *do*, you gotta let me redecorate. No grown man should be living in a bedroom papered with car calendar pages."

"For you, anything," Derrick agreed. "My wallet's in my jeans. Once you're done being a koala, help yourself."

It must have been a tempting offer, but Ginsberg didn't move.

Ah well, they had all the time in the world.

Or at least until 6 a.m. tomorrow morning. It wouldn't do to leave the guests hungry, after all.

Just the first early morning of the rest of their lives.

Explore more of *Bluewater Bay*:
riptidepublishing.com/titles/universe/bluewater-bay

Dear Reader,

Thank you for reading Heidi Belleau and Rachel Haimowitz's *The Burnt Toast B&B*!

We know your time is precious and you have many, many entertainment options, so it means a lot that you've chosen to spend your time reading. We really hope you enjoyed it.

We'd be honored if you'd consider posting a review—good or bad—on sites like **Amazon, Barnes & Noble, Kobo, Goodreads, Twitter, Facebook**, **Tumblr,** and your blog or website. We'd also be honored if you told your friends and family about this book. Word of mouth is a book's lifeblood!

For more information on upcoming releases, author interviews, blog tours, contests, giveaways, and more, please sign up for our weekly, spam-free newsletter and visit us around the web:

Newsletter: tinyurl.com/RiptideSignup
Twitter: twitter.com/RiptideBooks
Facebook: facebook.com/RiptidePublishing
Goodreads: tinyurl.com/RiptideOnGoodreads
Tumblr: riptidepublishing.tumblr.com

Thank you so much for Reading the Rainbow!

RiptidePublishing.com

This book could not have existed without the time and generosity of the many trans people—men, women, and nonbinary people alike—who volunteered their time and energy to help make this book the best rom-com we could write. Every question we asked on social media and Tumblr especially over the course of several months was met with literally *dozens* of thoughtful, honest answers and to everyone who contributed, we cannot thank you enough for your patience and your guidance, and we hope we did right by you all.

Special thanks, of course, must go to Mo Ranyart and Sam Schooler, who both took the time to serve as full beta readers for trans content, as well as all the other first-draft details beta readers regularly help with. Any and all remaining issues or inaccuracies are, of course, our own, but this all just goes to show that writing outside your own experience is totally achievable, because there's no shortage of people happy to help you make it right if only you reach out and ask.

We'd also like to thank our wonderful editors, KJ Charles and Caz Galloway; the keeper of the Bluewater Bay bible who helped us get all our details straight, Chris Muldoon; and all the other amazing authors and editors in the Bluewater Bay series who gave us such a fun sandbox to play in.

Rear Entrance Video series
Apple Polisher
Wallflower
Straight Shooter

The Professor's Rule series, with Amelia C. Gormley
Giving an Inch
An Inch at a Time
Inch by Inch
Every Inch of the Way
To the Very Last Inch

The Flesh Cartel serial, with Rachel Haimowitz
King of Dublin, with Lisa Henry
First Impressions. Second Chances
Blasphemer, Sinner, Saint, with Sam Schooler (in the *Bump in the Night* anthology)
Bliss, with Lisa Henry

With Violetta Vane
Mark of the Gladiator
Cruce de Caminos

Power Play: Resistance, with Cat Grant
Power Play: Awakening, with Cat Grant
Master Class (Master Class, #1)
SUBlime: Collected Shorts (Master Class, #2)
Counterpoint (Song of the Fallen, #1)
Crescendo (Song of the Fallen, #2)
Anchored (Belonging, #1)
The Flesh Cartel serial, with Heidi Belleau
Break and Enter, with Aleksandr Voinov

HEIDI BELLEAU was born and raised in small town New Brunswick, Canada. She now lives in the rugged oil-patch frontier of Northern BC with her husband, an Irish ex-pat whose long work hours in the trades leave her plenty of quiet time to write. She has a degree in history from Simon Fraser University with a concentration in British and Irish studies; much of her work centered on popular culture, oral folklore, and sexuality, but she was known to perplex her professors with unironic papers on the historical roots of modern romance novel tropes. (Ask her about Highlanders!) When not writing, you might catch her trying to explain British television to her newborn daughter or standing in line at the local coffee shop, waiting on her caramel macchiato.

You can visit her blog: www.heidibelleau.com, find her tweeting as @HeidiBelleau, email her at heidi.below.zero@gmail.com.

RACHEL HAIMOWITZ is an M/M erotic romance author and the Publisher of Riptide Publishing. She's also a sadist with a pesky conscience, shamelessly silly, and quite proudly pervish. Fortunately, all those things make writing a lot more fun for her . . . if not so much for her characters.

When she's not writing about hot guys getting it on (or just plain getting it; her characters rarely escape a story unscathed), she loves to read, hike, camp, sing, perform in community theater, and glue captions to cats. She also has a particular fondness for her very needy dog, her even needier cat, and shouting at kids to get off her lawn.

You can find Rachel at her website, rachelhaimowitz.com, on Tumblr at rachelhaimowitz.tumblr.com, and tweeting as @RachelHaimowitz. She loves to hear from folks, so feel free to drop her a line anytime at metarachel@gmail.com.

CPSIA information can be obtained at www.ICGtesting.com
Printed in the USA
LVOW07s0117240816

501564LV00005B/173/P